Never Cry "Arp!"

ALSO BY PATRICK F. MCMANUS

Kid Camping from Aaaaiii! to Zip

A Fine and Pleasant Misery

They Shoot Canoes, Don't They?

Never Sniff a Gift Fish

The Grasshopper Trap

Rubber Legs and White Tail-Hairs

The Night the Bear Ate Goombaw

Whatchagot Stew
(with Patricia "The Troll" McManus Gass)

Real Ponies Don't Go Oink!

The Good Samaritan Strikes Again

How I Got This Way

Never Cry "Arp!"

And Other Great Adventures

Patrick F. McManus

Henry Holt and Company

NEW YORK

Henry Holt and Company, LLC
Publishers since 1866
175 Fifth Avenue
New York, New York 10010
www.HenryHoltKids.com

Henry Holt® is a registered
trademark of Henry Holt and Company, LLC.

Distributed in Canada by H. B. Fenn and Company Ltd.

Library of Congress Cataloging-in-Publication Data
McManus, Patrick F.
Never Cry "Arp!"; and other great adventures /
Patrick F. McManus
p. cm.
Contents: Skunk dog—The mountain—Reading sign—Kid brothers and their practical applications—Never cry "Arp!"—Real ponies don't go Oink!—Secret places—A really nice blizzard—Cubs—Muldoon in love—Not long for this whirl—The right the bear ate goombaw.
1. Outdoor life—Juvenile Fiction. 2. Children's stories, American. 3. Humorous stories, American. [1. Outdoor life—Fiction. 2. Humorous stories. 3. Short stories.] I. Title.
PZ7.M47876Ne 1996 [Fic]—dc20 95-39420

ISBN 978-0-8050-4662-5

First Edition—1996

Printed in November 2009 in the United States of America
by R.R. Donnelley & Sons Company, Harrisonburg, Virginia

13 15 17 19 20 18 16 14

For my grandchildren:
Jake and Devon
Brookes and Jen
Joel, Elisa, and Daniel

Contents

To My Younger Readers:

These are stories about some of my adventures as a young boy growing up in the mountains of Idaho. Many of you, perhaps, are engaged right now in similar adventures, which will provide you with a rich source for your own stories for many years to come. I hope that is the case. A person needs his or her own adventures and his or her own stories.

I receive a great many letters from boys and girls, many of whom ask if my stories are true. The answer is "Yes!" Oh sure, I have varnished, stretched, and embroidered the original experiences somewhat. But that doesn't mean the stories aren't true. Stories always have their own truth.

Most of my stories are written with children in mind, and I try never to write over their heads, which I judge to have elevations of anywhere between three and five feet. If you're under three feet, you may occasionally have to stand on your tiptoes.

These stories have a simple purpose, and that is to make you laugh, even when you yourself sometimes feel like crying "Arp!"

Pat McManus
Clark Fork, Idaho
1995

Never Cry "Arp!"

1

Skunk Dog

WHEN I WAS A KID, I used to beg my mother to get me a dog.

"You've got a dog," she would say.

"No, I mean a real dog," I'd reply.

"Why, you've got Strange, and he's a real dog, more or less."

Strange was mostly less. He had stopped by to cadge a free meal off of us one day and found the pickings so easy he decided to stay on. He lived with us for ten years, although, as my grandmother used to say, it seemed like centuries. In all those years, he displayed not a single socially redeeming quality. If dogs were films, he'd have been X-rated.

I recall one Sunday when my mother had invited the new parish priest to dinner. Our dining room table was situated in front of a large window overlooking the front yard. During the first course, Strange passed by the window not once but twice, walking on his front legs but dragging his rear over the grass. His mouth was split in an ear-to-ear grin of sublime relief, and possibly of pride, in his discovery of a new treatment for embarrassing itch.

"Well, Father," Mom said in a hasty effort at distraction, "and how do you like our little town by now?"

"Hunh?" the pastor said, a fork full of salad frozen in mid-stroke as he gaped out the window at the disgusting spectacle. "Pardon me, what were you saying?"

During the next course, Strange appeared outside the window with the remains of some creature that had met its end sometime prior to the previous winter, no doubt something he had saved for just such a formal occasion. As he licked his chops in pretense of preparing to consume the loathsome object, Mom shot me a look that said, *"Kill that dog!"* I stepped to the door fully intending to carry out the order, but Strange ran off, snickering under his breath.

"More chicken, Father?" Mom asked.

"Thank you, I think not," the priest said, running a finger around the inside of his Roman collar, as if experiencing some welling of the throat.

Fortunately, the dinner was only four courses in length, ending before Strange could stage his grand finale. A female collie, three dead rats, and the entrails of a sheep were left waiting in the wings.

Mom said later she didn't know whether Strange was just being more disgusting than usual that day or had something against organized religion. In any case, it was a long while before the priest came to dinner again, our invitations invariably conflicting with funerals, baptisms, or his self-imposed days of fasting.

Strange was the only dog I've ever known who could belch at will. It was his idea of high comedy. If my mother had some of her friends over for a game of pinochle, Strange would slip into the house and slouch over to the ladies. Then he would emit a loud belch. Apparently, he mistook shudders of revulsion for a form of applause, because he would sit there on his haunches, grinning modestly up at the group and preparing an encore. "Stop, stop!" he would snarl, as I dragged him back outdoors. "They love me! They'll die laughing at my other routine! It'll have them on the floor!" I will not speak here of his other routine.

In general appearance, Strange could easily have been mistaken for your average brown-and-white mongrel with floppy ears and a shaggy tail, except that depravity was written all over him. He looked as if he sold dirty postcards to support an opium habit. His eyes spoke of having known the depths of degeneracy, and approving of them.

Tramps were his favorite people. If a tramp stopped by for a free meal at our picnic table and to case the place, Strange would greet him warmly, exchange bits of news about underworld connections, and leak inside information about the household: "They ain't got any decent jewelry, but the silver's not bad and there's a good radio in the living room." The tramp would reach down and scratch the dog behind the ears as a gesture of appreciation, and Strange would belch for him. Face wrinkled in disgust, the tramp would then hoist his bedroll and depart the premises, no doubt concerned about the reliability of food given him by a family that kept such a dog.

My friends at school often debated the attributes of various breeds of dogs. "I tend to favor black labs," I'd say, going on to recite the various characteristics I had recently excerpted from a *Field & Stream* dog column. Somehow my classmates got the impression that I actually owned a black lab and had personally observed these characteristics. While I was aware of the mistaken impression, I didn't feel it was my business to go around refuting all the rumors that happened to get started. Sooner or later, however, one of these friends would visit me at home. Strange would come out of his house and satisfy himself that the visitor wasn't a tramp in need of his counsel. That done, he would yawn, belch, gag, and return to his den of iniquity.

"That your uh dog?" the kid would ask.

"I guess so," I'd reply, embarrassed.

"Too bad," the kid would say. "I always thought you had a black lab."

"Naw, just him. But I'm planning on buying me a black lab pup first chance I get."

"I sure would," the kid would say, shaking his head.

As a hunting dog, Strange was a good deal worse than no dog. Nevertheless, he clearly thought of himself as a great hunting guide. "Fresh spoor," he would say, indicating a pine cone. "We can't be far behind him. And for gosh sakes shoot straight, because I judge from the sign he'll be in a bad mood!"

Chances of shooting any game at all with Strange along were nil. He had no concept of stealth. His standard hunting practice was to go through the woods shouting directions and advice to me and speculating loudly about the absence of game. I would have had more luck hunting with a rock band.

Strange did not believe in violence, except possibly in regard to chickens. He couldn't stand chickens. If a chicken walked by his house, Strange would rush out in a rage and tell the bird off and maybe even cuff it around a bit in the manner of early Bogart or Cagney. "You stupid chicken, don't ever let me catch you in dis neighborhood again, you hear?"

Some of our neighbors kept half-starved timber wolves for watchdogs. Occasionally one of these beasts would come loping warily through our yard and encounter Strange. Since Strange considered the whole world as his territory, he felt no particular obligation to defend this small portion of it. He would sit there, figuratively picking his teeth with a match, and stare insolently at the wolf, who was four times his size, its lip curled over glistening fangs, hackles raised, growls rumbling up from its belly. After a bit, the wolf would circle Strange, back away, and then lope on, occasionally casting a nervous glance back over its shoulder. "Punk!" Strange would mutter. Probably the reason none of these wolves ever attacked Strange was that they figured he was carrying a switchblade and maybe a blackjack.

Despite the peculiar passive side to his character, Strange did commit a single act of violence that was so terrible my mother actually considered selling the farm and moving us all to town. At the very least, she said, she was getting rid of Strange.

The episode began one warm spring evening when my grandmother sighted a skunk scurrying under our woodshed.

"He's probably the one that's been killing our chickens," Gram said. "I wouldn't be surprised but that he has his missus under there and they're planning a family. We'll be overrun with skunks!"

"Well, we'll just have to get him out from under the woodshed," Mom said. "Land sakes, a person can scarcely get a breath of fresh air in the backyard without smelling skunk. Maybe we should get Rancid Crabtree to come over and see what he can do about it."

"He'd certainly overpower the skunk smell," Gram said, "but I don't see that's any gain."

"What I mean is," Mom said, "maybe Rancid could trap the skunk or at least get it to leave. It's worth a try."

"I don't know," Gram said. "It just doesn't seem like a fair contest to me."

"Because Rancid uses guns and traps?" I asked.

"No, because the skunk has a brain!"

Gram and Rancid were not fond of each other.

The next day I was sent to tell Rancid we needed his expertise in extracting a skunk from under our woodshed. His face brightened at this news.

"Ha!" he said. "Thet ol' woman couldn't figure

out how to git a skonk out from under yore shed, so fust thang she does is start yelling fer ol' Crabtree! If thet don't beat all!"

"Actually, it was Mom who told me to come get you," I said.

"Oh. Wall, in thet case, Ah'll come. Jist keep the ol' woman outta ma ha'r."

When we arrived, Gram was standing out by the woodshed banging on a pot with a steel spoon and whooping and hollering. The old woodsman nudged me in the ribs and winked. I could tell he was going to get off one of his "good ones."

"Would you mind practicin' your drummin' and singin' somewhar else?" Rancid said to her. "Me and the boy got to git a skonk out from under thet shed."

If Gram could have given the skunk the same look she fired at Rancid, the creature would have been stunned if not killed outright. The glare had no effect on Rancid, however, since he was bent over laughing and slapping his knee in appreciation of his good one. It was, in fact, one of the best good ones I'd ever heard him get off, but I didn't dare laugh.

"All right, Bob Hope," Gram snapped. "Let's see how you get the skunk out from under there. Maybe if you stood upwind of it, that would do the trick!"

"Don't rile me, ol' woman, don't rile me," Rancid said. "Now, boy, go fetch me some newspapers. Ah'm gonna smoke thet critter outta thar."

"And burn down the shed most likely," Gram said.

"Ha!" Rancid said. "You thank Ah don't know how to smoke a skonk out from under a shed?"

Fortunately, the well and a bucket were close at hand and we were able to douse the fire before it did any more damage than blackening one corner of the building.

During these proceedings, Strange had emerged from his house and sat looking on with an air of bemusement. There was nothing he loved better than a ruckus.

"Maybe we should just let the skunk be," Mom said.

"Land sakes, yes!" Gram shouted at Rancid. "Before you destroy the whole dang farm!"

Rancid snorted. "No skonk's ever bested me yet, and this ain't gonna be the fust!"

After each failed attempt to drive out the skunk, Rancid seemed to become angrier and more frenzied. Furiously, he dug a hole on one side of the shed. Then he jammed a long pole in through the hole and flailed wildly about with it. No luck. He went inside the shed and jumped up and down on the floor with his heavy boots. Still no skunk emerged. At one point, he tried to crawl under the shed, apparently with the idea of entering into hand-to-gland combat with the skunk, but the shed floor was too low to the ground. Then he grabbed up the pole and flailed it wildly under the floor again. Next he dropped the pole and yelled at me, "Go git another batch of newspapers!"

"No, no, no!" screamed Mom.

"Leave the poor skunk alone," Gram yelled. "I'm startin' to become fond of the little critter!"

Rancid stood there panting and mopping sweat from his forehead with his arm. "Ah know what Ah'll do, Ah'll set a trap fer him! Should of did thet in the fust place. No skonk is gonna . . ."

At that moment, the skunk, no doubt taking advantage of the calm, or perhaps frightened by it, ran out from under the shed and made for the nearby brush.

"Ah figured thet little trick would work," Rancid said, although no one else was quite sure which trick he was speaking of. "And this way, there ain't no big stank, which is how Ah planned it."

Then Strange tore into the skunk.

The battle was short but fierce, with the skunk expending its whole arsenal as Strange dragged it about the yard, up the porch and down, into the woodshed and out, and through the group of frantically dispersing spectators. At last, coming to his senses, the dog dropped the skunk and allowed it to stagger off into the bushes.

Strange seemed embarrassed by his first and only display of heroism. "I don't know what came over me," he said, shaking. "I've got nothing against skunks!" Still, I couldn't help but be proud of him.

The skunk was gone, but its essence lingered on. The air was stiff with the smell of skunk for weeks afterwards.

"That dog has got to go," Mom said. But, of course, Strange refused to go, and that was that.

It was years before Strange was entirely free of the skunk odor. Every time he got wet, the smell came back in potent force.

"Phew!" a new friend of mine would say. "That your dog?"

"Yeah," I'd say, proudly, "he's a skunk dog."

2

The Mountain

"APRIL," THE POET WROTE, "is the cruelest month." Boy, no kidding! If I had read that poem while in third grade at Delmore Blight Grade School, I might very well have said, "How true! How true!" Although it's more likely I would have said, "Do I really have to read this stupid poem?"

Outside the grimy windows of third grade, April was dissolving the last lingering stains of winter. Inside, however, Miss Goosehart was stretching us pupils on the rack of the multiplication table, a fiendish device once used to torture young children. April was slipping from our grasp. Flowers were bursting into bloom, trees were leafing out, and the sap was rising, namely one Milton Clinker, to give the answer to four times seven. Who cared about four times seven, anyway? Only a sap like Clinker would want to multiply while all outdoors filled up with April.

Miss Goosehart cranked up the rack another notch. "Pat, would you take one of your wild guesses at three times six?"

I scratched my head in a show of concentration. Crazy Eddie Muldoon, who sat behind me, leaned forward and whispered something. I thought maybe it was the answer. But it was, "Saturday, let's climb the mountain."

Eddie was so far gone with April he didn't even realize it was my turn on the rack. He wasn't called Crazy Eddie for nothing.

"Give me a hint," I said to Miss Goosehart. "How many letters does it have?"

Had Eddie really said, "Let's climb the mountain"? What a terrific idea! My heart did a handspring at the very thought. "Okay," I whispered back. Eddie groaned. Miss Goosehart now had him on the rack, trying to wrench out the answer to seven times seven. It was ghastly.

The mountain Eddie and I intended to climb reared up abruptly from the valley about a mile from our farm. At night, in the glow of the moon, the mountain took on the shape of a sleeping dragon, the high, ragged peak forming the hump of its back; a long, descending ridge was its neck, and another knob of mountain was its head. The head of the dragon rested on the valley floor not far from Delmore Blight Grade School. It was easy to imagine the dragon awakening one night, stretching out its neck, and gobbling up the school in a single bite. In the morning the only evidence of what had happened would be a gaping hole in the ground and the smile on my face.

The dragon lived only at night. Daylight revealed a solid, no-nonsense mountain, with a craggy granite peak, sheer cliffs, a crosshatching of crevices and ledges, and, lower down, thick forest.

The mountain talked to me. I don't mean to imply that we held long philosophical conversations, but even as a small boy, sitting on the back steps of my house, I could hear it calling: "Pat! Pat! Come climb me! It will be fun! And I won't try to kill you, as I do some folks!"

On an April Saturday at the age of eight, I learned that mountains don't always tell the truth.

Before setting out for the mountain, Crazy Eddie and I told our mothers that we were going for a hike. It seemed like the only decent thing to do.

"Don't you go barefooted," my mother ordered. "It's too early in the year, and you'll catch your death. Stay away from the crick, because it's too high and you might fall in and drown. Don't tease the Guttenbergs' bull, because he might gore you to death. Don't cut yourself with your jackknife because you might bleed to death. Don't wander around in the woods, because you might get lost and starve to death." She stopped to catch her breath and search her memory. "Oh yes, don't climb any tall trees because you might fall to your death."

Mothers can be depressing. Mom couldn't recall any disasters with me and a mountain, and I saw no reason to give her further cause for worry by going into a lot of unnecessary detail about the hike. My mother was downright permissive compared with Eddie's parents. On Saturday mornings at his house, the family had to get up an hour early to run through the list of don'ts for Eddie and still have time enough to get the milking done by eight.

Eddie, as I expected, was late getting to my house. He looked good, swaggering into the yard, his eyes bright with the anticipation of great adventure. His broken arm had healed nicely. I envied the scar at his hairline, the result of his not having ducked quite low enough as we threw ourselves under the Guttenbergs' fence, and just in time, too. (There's nothing quite so disgusting as getting bull slobber sprayed all over you.) I thought maybe Eddie was concealing his limp from me, but apparently the fall from the cottonwood tree hadn't done any lasting damage. He seemed fit, which was more than I could say for his parents, the two most nervous people I'd ever known. As Eddie said, they probably drank too much coffee.

"Your folks skipped 'Don't mountain climb,' didn't they?" I said, grinning.

"Yep," Eddie said. "Never even occurred to them. They hit everything else, except dirt-clod throwing. The lump on your head go away?"

"More or less," I said. "It was my fault. I would have ducked faster if I'd known you were gonna charge my foxhole. You ready?"

"Sure," Eddie said. "Let's go!"

An hour later we were working our way up the lower slope of the mountain. Here and there the April sun had slipped in among the trees and incited a riot of buttercups. We each picked a handful of the little yellow flowers and put them in our shirt pockets to take home to our mothers. For some reason, mothers seemed thrilled by these little squished balls of withered flowers. So what the heck. The effort more than paid for itself with the PR spinoff. Say you were found guilty of getting home five hours late and had been sentenced to some whacks, the number to be determined by how long it took the parent's arm to feel as though it were about to fall off; the idea was to haul out the pitiful little bouquet and present it to your mother just before the penalty was to be executed. Nine times out of ten the bouquet got you a stay of execution. Wilted bouquets of wildflowers were not only good PR but excellent insurance.

"You got enough buttercups?" I asked.

"Yeah," Eddie said. "These should do the trick. Anyway, we probably won't get home that late."

We climbed the mountain for an hour, expecting always to reach the top at the next rise. But there was always another rise and another after that and still another. Finally we broke free of the sloping forests and could survey the valley down below. The familiar fields and pastures had taken on a new look, shaping themselves into intricate rectangular patterns of spring browns and greens. Mouse-size cars scurried up and down the roads.

The climbing had now become more difficult. Eddie, a born leader (the worst kind), took charge of planning our ascent. It seemed to me his motive was not to find the easiest route but to test our character. When we came to a rocky knob we could just as well have walked around, he insisted that we make a frontal assault on it, finding little cracks and protuberances with which to pull ourselves upward. When I complained, he said, "This is the way mountain climbing is done. Any sissy could walk around."

Now we were high up on the mountain. The cars below had shrunk to the size of ladybugs; cows and horses appeared no larger than ants.

"It's getting steeper," Eddie said, panting.

"And colder," I said, shivering.

"That means we're nearly to the top," Eddie said.

"I don't know," I said. "We've been 'nearly to the top' fifteen times already. Maybe we should turn back."

"Only a sissy would turn back," Eddie said.

"I'm not turning back," I said.

"Okay," Eddie said.

Among the patchwork of fields below, I could see my own little tiny warm house. It called to me in the same way the mountain had. "Turn back," it called. "Turn back."

"I'm not turning back," I muttered.

"Okay, okay," Eddie said. "I didn't say you were."

Eddie no longer had to seek out difficult routes. *Every* route had become difficult. Once we had to drop into a deep ravine, losing altitude we had already paid for, only to have to buy it again, inch by inch, foot by foot. On the shaded side of a ridge we encountered deep drifts of snow, streams of ice water gushing from beneath them. The April sun had rotted the drifts, and at every step we sank in almost to our waists, the gritty snow stinging our legs raw.

Once, as we stopped to rest against a gnarled, stunted tree, my pants freezing to my legs, my lungs aching, I stared out over the empty space to where Delmore Blight Grade School snuggled up against the edge of town. Old Delmore Blight Grade School, I thought. Well, this is a heck of a lot better than being *there*. The thought gave me strength to go on.

Late in the afternoon, finally, the jagged peak of the mountain came into view. There was no mistaking it. A few hundred yards more and we would reach the ridge that led up to the peak. After that, the summit would be as good as ours!

But our ascent now appeared to be blocked. A twenty-foot cliff rose directly above us. To get around it we would have to drop far back down the mountain and climb up again by another route. I knew now that we would have to turn back. Only a crazy person would try to scale the cliff.

"Boy, this looks dangerous," Eddie said. "Great! I bet a lot of guys would chicken out right now. Here, let me give you a boost."

I hauled myself over the lip of the cliff only to discover a great expanse of rock sloping steeply toward me. Water bright with sunlight trickled in tiny streams down the face of the rock. There was no going back now. I began to crawl on my belly up the slippery slab of granite—five feet, twenty feet, fifty feet. I thought: *Just about got it made. Then I can watch ol' Eddie climb up here. Ha! Bet he'll be scared. Just a bit more and I can reach for the upper edge of the slab. Only ten inches to go! Six inches! Three inches! Oh-oh, I slipped back an inch. Better get a foot in a crack or something. Still slipping. Still slipping! Dig my fingernails into the rock! No! Wait! What's happening? I can't stop sliding! I'm going too faaaaaaaaaaaaast!*

Buttons flew off my jacket and shirt like shrapnel. The knees ripped out of my pants. I felt as though I were leaving a streak of hide all the way down the rock. I whipped over on my back to see where I was going. Then I saw where! I tried to whip back on my stomach so I wouldn't have to see. But it was too late. I shot off over the edge of the cliff.

WHUFFF!—I saw green. I had flown spread-eagle right into a scrawny but merciful fir tree. It bent over and deposited me with a plop on a patch of snow.

I lay on my back, eyes closed, letting life drain back into me. Except for a few miscellaneous patches of missing clothing and hide, I seemed all right. Presently I heard a scrabbling in the rocks off to one side. I knew it must be Eddie. So I played dead to teach him a good lesson. He didn't say anything, but I could sense him looking down at me. I held my breath so he couldn't see me breathe. I could feel him studying me intently, wondering how he could explain the fatal accident. ("I tried to talk Pat out of it, but he wouldn't listen. Can I go play now?") Peeking from beneath my eyelids, I saw him bend over me. What was he doing? Checking to see if I might still be alive? Eddie set a large rock on my chest. He put another rock next to it, and then another. He was burying me.

"Stop!" I yelled. "I'm alive!"

"I knew you were still in there," Eddie said. "I saw you peeking out from under your eyelids. I just wanted to practice burying a person, in case I ever have to. Did you know you're bleeding through your shirt?"

"Just a scratch," I said. I had always wanted to say that.

"Good," Eddie said. "But next time you get up near the top of that slab of rock, grab hold of a branch or something. Otherwise, you'll just slide off again. C'mon, I'll give you a boost to get you started."

I stared hard at Eddie. "Forget it," I said. "I'm not climbing back up there."

"But we're so near the top!" Eddie cried. "You can't quit now. Look, you can even see the peak."

Against my better judgment, I looked at the peak, that ragged, twisted point of granite gleaming against the dark blue of the April sky, so beautiful and majestic that the mere sight of it could make a person dizzy with awe. Suddenly I knew what I had to do, and I did it.

"Cripes!" Eddie wailed. "Not on my shoes!"

I wiped my mouth on my torn, bloody sleeve. "Sorry about your shoes, Eddie, but I'm going back down the mountain. You can climb to the top by yourself if you want."

"I will, too!" Eddie said.

I limped back the way we had come. Then I heard Eddie running after me. "But I'll climb it some other time," he said. "Now I'd better help you."

"To do what?" I asked.

"To pick buttercups," Eddie said. "When your mom sees those clothes, you're going to need a whole lot more buttercups than you've got."

3

Reading Sign

BACK WHEN I WAS A KID, the mark of a true woodsman was his ability to read sign. Knowing this, many persons trying to pass themselves off as woodsmen would make a great show of staring at sign for a few minutes and then offering up profound remarks about it:

"I'd judge from this broken twig that we're about ten minutes behind a herd of mule deer, most of them yearlings or does, but there's one big fella I'd guess to be a trophy buck. You'll know him when you see him 'cause he favors his left front leg when he's running flat out and . . ."

The only way to deal with a person like that was to walk over, look down, and say, "For heaven's sake, so that's where I dropped my lucky twig! The amazing thing is, I broke it three months ago and it still works!" You then picked up the twig, put it in your pocket, and strolled away.

My cousin Buck was one of these impostors. Even though I was several years younger than Buck, sign was serious business to me and I spent long hours reading about it and studying it first-hand and trying to find out what it meant and whether it was sign at all or maybe just an accident. Buck, on the other hand, couldn't concentrate on any subject longer than fifteen seconds unless it wore a dress and smelled of perfume, which sign seldom if ever did. Still, every so often I had to endure his hauling me out to the woods to instruct me on how to read sign.

"Hey, looky here," he would hiss at me. "Elk sign!"

Now, any fool could see that the sign was not that of an elk but the handiwork of a mule who stood nearby with a smile on his face and a snicker in his voice. If I hadn't been smarter than I looked, I would have pointed that fact out to Buck. But not wishing to have my head thumped, I said, "Yes! Elk! Elk! I can see now they were elk!"

Thumping your head was Buck's way of proving to you that he could read sign.

If I, on the other hand, happened to discover some fresh deer sign, Buck would always dismiss my find with a shrug of his shoulders and the profound bit of wisdom: "You can't eat sign."

He lived to regurgitate those words.

One frosty November morn Buck had dragged me out deer hunting with him. I wasn't old enough yet to carry a rifle, but Buck needed someone along to brag to about how he could read sign. We were cruising down a back road in Buck's old car, listening to Gene Autry on the radio and looking for deer. (Buck believed the way to hunt deer was to drive up and down roads; that's the sort of woodsman he was.) For breakfast I had brought along some chocolate-covered peanuts in my jacket pocket, and every so often I'd sneak one into my mouth so Buck wouldn't see it and demand a share. There was some fool notion in those days that if someone saw you with something good to eat, all he had to do was yell "divvies" at you and then you had to share with him. If you didn't share with somebody when he yelled "divvies" at you, he got to beat you up and take it all—but only if he was bigger than you were. If he was smaller, he could yell "divvies" till the sun went down and you didn't have to share with him. In that way, I suppose, it was an equitable system. But I digress.

So anyway, there we were driving down the back road, and all at once Buck hit the brakes and yelled out, "Deer tracks!" Sure enough, even from where I now sat, wedged up under the dashboard, I could see that sometime during the past six months a deer had come sliding and bounding through the soft dirt of a high bank above the road. As soon as the car had slid to a stop, we jumped out, Buck breathlessly thumbing cartridges into his rifle, and rushed over to examine the tracks. All the while, Buck was making sure he got full credit for spotting the tracks.

"I told you they was deer tracks, and you didn't believe me, did you?" he whispered, his voice shrill with excitement.

"I believed you, Buck."

"Hell, we musta been drivin' past fifty miles an hour and I looks out and I says to you, 'There's some deer tracks!' Now didn't I say that?"

"That's what you said, Buck."

We looked at the tracks. Buck got down on his knees and felt the edges of the tracks, apparently to see if they were still warm. Then he bent over and sniffed them! It was almost too much to bear for a serious student of deer tracks. Any fool could see those tracks were so old they could have been classified as fossils. The deer who made them no doubt had since known a long and happy life and finally expired at a ripe old age.

"They fresh, Buck?" I asked.

Buck stood up and tugged at his wispy beard as he studied the tracks. "I'd say he went through here, oh, about a half-hour before daylight."

"Gee," I said, stifling a yawn. "We just missed him, hunh? Dang. If we had just been a few minutes earlier, hunh, Buck?"

"Yep," Buck said. "Well, win some, lose some."

While I was racking my brain trying to think of some that Buck had won, a terrible idea occurred to me. And the instant the idea occurred, I implemented it. Even after thirty years and more I am still ashamed of pulling it on Buck. That I am still convulsed with laughter upon recalling the expression on his face is even more despicable. Only the desire to ease my conscience compels me to confess the deed. What I did—oh, I shudder still to think of it—was to take a handful of the chocolate-covered peanuts and sprinkle them on the ground by my feet.

"Hey, Buck," I said, pointing. "Sign. Looks fresh, too."

Buck looked at me in disgust and shook his shaggy head. "How many times I got to tell ya: Ya can't eat sign!"

At that, I reached down, picked up a chocolate-covered peanut, snapped it into the air, and caught it in my mouth.

Buck's jaw dropped halfway to his belt buckle.

For years afterwards, Buck couldn't stand the sight of chocolate-covered peanuts. Offer him one and his upper lip would flutter like a broken window shade. Sure, when ol' Buck figured out the trick I'd played on him, he thumped my head until both of us were worn out, but that didn't change the obvious truth: He just wasn't a proper woodsman.

Much of my early knowledge about sign was gained from reading books and magazine articles. These usually included drawings of the tracks of various wild animals, and all you had to do was memorize the shape and the number of toes and so on to be able to identify the track out in the wilds. I spent endless hours at this sort of study, but it was well worth the effort. For one thing, it taught me about true friendship. If you were out with one of your friends in the woods, you could point to a set of tracks and say, "Look, lynx tracks."

"Gee," the friend would say in a properly appreciative tone. If he didn't say that or an equivalent expression, he wasn't your friend.

Now, if you followed the lynx tracks and at the other end of them found a skunk waddling along, you would say to your friend, studying him closely, "Sometimes skunks make lynx tracks, did you know that?"

"No, I didn't," he might reply. "That's really interesting." Such a reply could mean only two things: This guy was impossibly stupid, or he was a *really* good friend.

Strangely enough, many of the magazine articles on sign were written by a lady. Her underlying principle was that wild animals were actors on the stage of the great outdoors. If you could read the scripts, namely their tracks in the snow, you could decipher the plot. A typical plot would go like this: Rabbit tracks are crossing the snow from one direction and coyote tracks from another. The two sets of tracks intersect at the base of a tree. Only the coyote tracks continue on from the tree. Hmmmmmmmmmmmm. How did the rabbit get away from the tree without making any tracks? Did he climb the tree? The mystery was almost mind-boggling. The author of these articles could take an hour's walk through the snow and encounter a dozen fascinating little dramas, none of which, I might add, were ever comedies.

I hate to admit it, but at a certain age I was intrigued by these articles and was forever searching the snowy countryside for evidence of little wildlife dramas. Unfortunately, most of the dramas I encountered went about like this: Rabbit tracks emerge from thicket, go under barbwire fence, mess around in a patch of blackberry brambles, cross a creek over thin ice, go under another barbwire fence, mosey back across the thin ice, meander through the blackberry brambles again, pass under another barbwire fence, and go back into the thicket. That would be it. Although the drama itself might be deadly dull, following the "script" around the countryside could be fraught with pain, danger, and excitement. Several times I nearly froze to death in my wet clothes while rushing home to bandage my scratches and cuts and to dig out the stickers.

Where I really learned to read sign was from the old woodsman Rancid Crabtree. Rancid didn't care a hoot about reading little woodland dramas. To him, sign was not a form of entertainment but an essential element in a complex scheme that he had devised to make working for a living unnecessary. About the only things Rancid needed money for were a few clothes, rifle and shotgun shells, salt and pepper, some gas for his old truck, chewin' tobacco, and his medicine, which a local pharmacist, a Colt .45 stuffed in the waistband of his pants, delivered at night in quart-sized Mason jars. These commodities required cash, particularly the medicine. Rancid acquired his cash by running a little trap line each winter. And successful trapping required a rather extensive knowledge of sign. The intensity and seriousness with which Rancid studied sign can be fully appreciated only by realizing that to him it was virtually the same thing as tobacco and medicine. To Rancid, sign was a matter of ultimate concern.

A stroll with Rancid through the woods was a course in post-graduate study in reading sign. "B'ar," he would say, pointing to the ground as we walked along. "Porky-pine . . . bobcat . . . skonk . . ." And so on. One day we were going along in this fashion and he pointed down and said, "Snake."

"Snake?" I said to myself, glancing down. "This is a new . . . SNAKE!" My bare foot was descending toward the fat, frantic reptile. Despite my precarious posture, I managed to execute a successful lift-off before coming into actual contact with the creature. While involved in this effort, I left my vocal cords unattended and they took advantage of their moment of freedom to get off a loud and startling shriek. Upon hearing this, Rancid leaped to the conclusion that he had misjudged the snake as being a member of a benevolent sect and immediately began to curse and hop about and flail the earth with his walking stick. It was all pretty exciting, and Rancid was more than a little annoyed when he found out the snake hadn't taken a bite out of me after all.

"Gol-dang," he said, "don't never scream like thet ag'in fer no reason. Let the thang at least git a taste of you 'fer you starts hollerin' like you's bein' et. Now tarn loose maw ha'r and neck and git down offen maw shoulders!"

Kid Brothers and Their Practical Application

I ALWAYS THOUGHT it would be nice to have a kid brother. All I ever had was an older sister, who at best wasn't much fun and at worst was dreadful. It is a terrible thing to have a sister who is bigger and stronger than you are. Say you're hanging out in the yard with some of the guys, explaining to them exactly what you'll do to the school bully if he "pulls any of that stuff" with you, and suddenly your older sister comes out on the porch and bellows at you to get in the house and help with the dishes. You respond with a cutting remark that gets a chuckle out of the guys. Your sister then bounds off the porch, throws three of the guys to the ground, grabs you, twists your arm up between your shoulder blades, and marches you into the house on your tiptoes. That sort of thing can ruin a guy's image. Older sisters can be bad.

But suppose you had a kid brother, say about three years younger than yourself. Think of the fun you could have with him. You could lock him in the basement, say, and turn off all the lights, and he's down there screaming and yelling and crying, claiming that he just felt an icy hand on his neck. See, he doesn't know it's your icy hand, because you sneaked back into the basement and grabbed him by the neck. And sometimes, when there wasn't anything else to do, you could practice your tying-up techniques on him. (Kids realize early on that when they get to be adults they'll have to spend a lot of time tying people up, so it's important they get practice. A kid brother would be perfect for this.) One of the best things of all you could do with a kid brother would be to say, "Beat it, kid," whenever he tried to hang out with you and the guys, and he would have to beat it, because if he doesn't he knows you'll lock him in the basement again.

You could teach your kid brother all kinds of stuff, too, just to help him out. You could teach him how to build a campfire and pitch a tent and bait a hook and make a slingshot or a bow-and-arrow. Maybe he wouldn't want to learn any of this stuff, but that wouldn't make any difference, because he would be smaller than you, and you could teach him anyway. What's the use of knowing something if you don't have anybody around to teach it to?

Whenever you weren't tying him up or locking him in the basement or teaching him things or telling him to beat it, you could find lots of other uses for a kid brother. You could send him on errands, real or imaginary, play the old snipe-trapping trick on him, use him as a test pilot on rafts and go-carts to see if they were safe, any number of things. I really missed having a kid brother.

Several of my friends had kid brothers, and more or less took them for granted. I envied them but never let on. The accepted attitude toward kid brothers was to regard them as a nuisance. I personally felt that my associates never exploited their kid brothers to the full potential, but I didn't feel it would be appropriate for me to offer advice. That would be like a man who had never owned a dog lecturing his friends on how to train their dogs. (Actually, this is a favorite pastime of persons who have never owned a dog, but why put myself in a bad mood by dwelling on it?) Many was the time when one of my friends complained there was nothing to do that I wanted to suggest we tie up his kid brother in the basement and turn off the lights and listen to him yell. But I never did. It would have been different if I'd had one of my own, so we could have taken turns using each other's kid brother for a project. You take advantage of a person if you can't return the favor in kind, and that's not right.

My friend Retch Sweeney had two kid brothers, Erful and Verman. Erful was about the right age for a kid brother, three years younger than ourselves, and we got quite a bit of use out of him. Verman was too young and small to be of much value. Besides, he had a runny nose all the time, and it made you sick to look at him, let alone to actually touch him. A runny nose is a great defense mechanism if you're a kid brother. Even now it turns my stomach, just remembering little Verman. I thought of him as the Nose.

Erful Sweeney was a chunky toe-head, meaning that he had a head that looked like a toe. I don't know if he was born that way or whether Retch had done the shaping on the kid's head after he was older. To call Erful homely was to flatter him extravagantly.

As a kid brother, Erful seemed just about perfect to me, but Retch regarded him as a large fat tick embedded in his life. Throughout my youthful association with Retch, Erful stands out in my memory as a constant, lurking presence. In the early years at least, he had a low whining threshold, which could get on a person's nerves. Retch and I would be out in the barn shooting baskets in the haymow, and there would be this background sound of Erful whining, "C'mon, you guys, let me play. If you don't, I'm gonna tell!" This was Erful's power whine—"I'm gonna tell!" Sometimes it would make me laugh right out loud, it was so ludicrous. Retch was usually in such big-time trouble with his folks that Erful's telling on him for not letting him play was like giving a parking ticket to John Dillinger. "Beat it, kid," Retch would say, "before I tie you up in the basement and turn off all the lights."

"Hey, good idea," I'd say.

"I'll tell!" Erful would whine.

Erful had a face that only a mother could love, and I don't think his mother cared all that much for it. She seemed always trying to get his face out of the house.

"Where you boys going now?" she demanded of us one day.

"Down to the river fishin'," Retch said. "And I ain't takin' Erful."

"You most certainly are taking Erful! You just wait until he finishes his peanut butter and jelly sandwich. Erful, hurry up and eat so you can go fishing with Pat and Retch. Wash your toe—uh—your face first."

"C'mon, Ma, don't be mean," Retch said. "Why do I have to take Erful everywhere?"

"Because he's your brother, that's why. Besides, this will give Erful a chance to use the new fish pole he got for his birthday."

"Yeah!" Erful said. "And my new reel! Wow! Wait up, guys, till I go get my new fish pole and reel."

Then Verman piped up, wiping his sleeve across his nose, "Can I go fishin' with Pat and Retch, too, Ma?"

Mrs. Sweeney looked at her youngest son, the Nose. "No, you're—gag—too little to go down to the—gag—river. Then again—gag—maybe not."

We went out and got on our bikes. The standard procedure for the older guys was to ride off as fast as possible and leave the kid brother far behind, whining loudly, "Wait up! You're going too fast!" We always got a chuckle out of this particular whine, since the kid brother obviously thought we were unaware we were going too fast for him. Once out of sight of our pursuer, we would hide and let him race on by, still howling, "Wait up, guys! You're going too fast!" even though we were no longer even in sight. Kid brothers were dumb.

On this particular day, Retch tried to vary the routine a little. Before we rode off from his house, he said to Erful, "Hey, Erful, let's run down to the basement a second. I got some candy hidden away down there. Don't that sound good?"

"Naw," Erful said. "You're not getting me down in the basement! Whine whine."

Usually, Erful wasn't that suspicious. As I told Retch later, the trick might have worked if he hadn't been holding the length of clothesline rope right out where Erful could see it.

All we could do was ride away from Erful, hide until he went whining by, and then go off fishing at some remote place along the river where he wasn't likely to find us, in other words the standard procedure, which was all right but not nearly so efficient as leaving him tied up in the basement.

After we had ditched Erful, Retch and I rode up to China Bend, which was good fishing but a little dangerous, the sort of place where you wouldn't want to fall off the bank or jump in and try to net a fish that was too big just to jerk up onto the bank. Oh, if it was a really big fish, of course you would go in, but it was the sort of risk you wouldn't take for anything under sixteen inches, particularly with the current as cold and churning as it was now.

After a couple of hours, Retch and I had caught half a dozen smallish trout, nothing to get excited about, and were just enjoying the peace and quiet of the river, when all at once Erful came panting up on his bicycle.

"Gee, guys, you lost me," he said. "I guess you wondered what happened to me, but I've been looking all over for you. Bet you thought I went back home."

"Yeah, sort of," Retch said. "When we couldn't find you, we just came up here and started fishin'. I said to ol' Pat here, 'I wonder what became of Erful,' and Pat said, 'Oh, he probably went home.'"

"Nope. I just hunted till I found you. Now I want to try out my new fish pole."

"Yeah, well, this isn't a good place to do it," Retch said. "The bank's startin' to cave away and you might fall in."

"Oh sure, tell me about it!" Erful whined. "You're just tryin' to get rid of me! I'm gonna tell, too!" With that, he stepped over to the edge of the bank, which instantly caved in with him. Shrieking, he clawed at the loosening sod around him, his feet already being swept downstream by the greedy current. Ignoring the impulse to laugh at this comical spectacle, I lunged heroically toward the bank, grabbed Erful by his toe-head, and hauled him to safety. (Later I thought how lucky that it had been Erful the bank had caved in with and not Verman, because the Nose probably would have had to go into the river.)

In all the excitement, it took us several seconds to realize that Erful's new fish pole had plopped right into the deepest hole at China Bend.

"Well, that was one fish pole that didn't last

long," Retch said. "Goodbye, birthday fish pole. Maybe next birthday you'll get another one, Erful. That's only a year away. Twelve long months that you'll have to use your old fish pole. I guess you'll pay attention to what I tell you from now on."

Erful emitted a howl of gloom and despair so pitiful that Retch and I had to laugh. He then got on his bike and pedaled off toward home, sounding like a broken fire siren.

"Stupid kid," Retch said, untying the laces on his shoes. "Serves him right, losing his new fish pole." He pulled his sweatshirt off over his head. "I don't know why my folks bother to keep him around." He undid his belt and stepped out of his pants. "He's just a nuisance." Retch then dived into the cold, swirling waters of China Bend.

On his fourth dive, Retch finally found the fish pole and swam downstream to a place where he could claw his way up the bank. He was blue and shivering. He tossed the fish pole on the ground and started putting his pants back on. He didn't say anything for a while, because he was so embarrassed, and also because his teeth were chattering so hard I wouldn't have been able to understand him anyway.

After a bit he said sheepishly, "I hope you won't tell the guys about this. You know, about me going in the river after Erful's fish pole. It was all he got for his birthday, and . . ."

"Not me," I said. "I'm not going to tell anybody about it."

And I didn't. When you see a character flaw of that magnitude suddenly revealed in your best friend, you're certainly not about to spread it around.

Never Cry "Arp!"

I HAVE LONG MAINTAINED that it is not the fish caught nor the game shot that makes the outdoor life so satisfying but the miseries endured in the course of those endeavors. I was first introduced to the satisfaction of outdoor miseries by my good friend Crazy Eddie Muldoon, who, at age eight, was a sort of magnet to injuries. It was almost as though Eddie scheduled his injuries for the day when he got up in the morning.

8:00	Stub big toe of left foot.
8:35	Step on rusty nail with right foot.
9:05	Get stung over left eye by bee.
10:30	Run sliver in hand while whittling.
10:35	Cut finger while whittling.
11:00	Twist ankle jumping off pigpen fence.

11:22	Get tick embedded behind left ear.
12:00	Lunch.
1:15	Get stung by nettles.
2:00	Get bitten by the Petersons' dog.

And so on throughout the day. I never knew there were so many injuries to be had until I met Crazy Eddie. There were burns, bangs, bites, breaks, cuts, conks, fractures, gouges, hits, knocks, punctures, pulls, pinches, scrapes, scratches, smashes, stings, stubs, strains, sprains, whacks, wrenches, and wallops.

And more. By the end of a day, Eddie would acquire most of them. He would go home with a series of tear flows recorded in the dirt on his face, like the various flows of lava from a volcano. There would be the eleven-o'clock twisted-ankle flow stopped just short of the two-o'clock dogbite flow. A geologist could read the day's events on Eddie's face.

It was Eddie who taught me never to cry over an injury, no matter how painful. He said you were just supposed to laugh it off. For instance, once Eddie was banging two big rocks together to see if there were any gold nuggets inside, and one of his fingers slipped between the rocks. The distinctive sound still sticks in my mind: *WHOCK WHOCK WHOCK whib "Aaaaaaaiiiiii!"* Eddie hunched over and hopped around with his flat finger clutched in his crotch, performing a variation of the adult outdoorsman's traditional crouch hop, but more agile and much faster, like a basketball being dribbled at blurring speed. He also emitted strange, high-pitched sounds.

With much concern, I studied Eddie's face for signs of tears. "Hey, you're crying, Eddie. You got tears runnin' down your face."

"Hiii-yiiii! Ow ow!" he yelled. "No I ain't! Owwwww! Ha ha! Owwwww! Waaaa! Ha ha! See, I'm laughing it off. Oww! Waaa! Ha ha! Haaiiii!"

"I think you're crying."

"Nope, I'm not."

"Oh, sorry, I thought you was."

"Nope."

I never knew Eddie when he had all of his fingernails whole and healthy. Most of them would be in various stages of coming or going, either shiny pink little nubbins or hideous black things.

"Hey, this fingernail is about to come off," he would tell me. "Want to see me peel it?"

"Sure."

"Ouch! There. What did you think of that? I got another one about ready to peel, too. I'll let you know when it's time."

I never told Eddie, because I didn't want to hurt his feelings, but watching him peel off his fingernails wasn't all that entertaining. It lacked the suspense of his slowly unwrapping a bandage so I could see one of his nastier wounds.

Usually, Eddie accumulated his injuries sequentially. But on one occasion he got them all at once. We were roaring down a steep hill on our bicycles when Eddie's bike chain ate his pant leg. At the same time, a hornet traveling at supersonic speed hit him right between the eyes. Eddie was knocked backwards right off his bike. He and the bike bounced and smashed and crashed on down the hill, until at last they both racked up in a pile against a signpost. I braked to a stop on one of his arms. Eddie didn't seem to notice. He and the bike looked as if they had been wadded up and tossed out the window of a passing car. Well, I thought, if I'm ever going to see Eddie cry, this is it.

He didn't cry, though. He just lay there in a tangle of bicycle, saying something that sounded like "Arp arp arp." I pulled his pants leg loose from the bike chain, got him astraddle of the rear-fender carrier on my bike, and pedaled him toward his house.

"Feel like playing some more, or you want to go home, Eddie?" I asked him.

"Arp arp arp," he replied. So I took him home.

I dumped him off the bike in his yard and he just lay there on the grass. I figured I could leave him there, and sooner or later his mother would find him. If I stayed, I'd have to explain how it all happened and how it wasn't my fault and all the other nonsense required on such occasions.

"Arp arp arp," Eddie said to me.

"Oh, all right," I said. "I'll go tell your mom." For all his shortcomings, Eddie had a way with words.

I knocked on the door, and Mrs. Muldoon called out for me to come into the kitchen. She smiled at me, wiping her hands on her apron. "Land sakes, Patrick, where did you get all those scratches on your face?"

"Eddie and me was climbing a thorn apple tree."

"Well, you're certainly a mess."

"Yeah, but wait until you see Eddie."

"Oh, that boy! He's always getting himself so banged up. But he never cries, does he?"

"Nope. But he says 'Arp arp arp' a lot."

"'Arp arp arp'? Say, would you like a cookie and a glass of milk?"

"Yes, ma'am."

Mrs. Muldoon poured two glasses of milk and set them on the table with a little pile of sugar cookies beside each. I dipped a cookie in my glass of milk and bit off the soggy portion. There was a well-established technique for eating sugar cookies with milk. The cookie was too big around to fit all the way into the glass. So you dipped an edge of it as far as it would reach into the milk. Then you ate off that edge. Next, you turned the cookie over and dipped the opposite edge in the milk and ate it off. Now the cookie was narrow enough to fit all the way down into the glass, and you could dip it and eat it in two bites.

Mrs. Muldoon smiled at me. I could tell she knew a skilled milk-and-sugar-cookie eater when she saw one. "Where's Eddie?" she asked. "Isn't he coming in?"

"Oh, I nearly forgot," I said. "Eddie got hurt."

"Oh dear, that boy! He is always getting himself so banged up. What is it this time? His big toe? Another finger?"

I expertly finished off a second sugar cookie. "I don't know for sure," I said, "but to me it looks pretty much like all of him."

Mrs. Muldoon walked to the door and looked out. "Good heavens! Eddieeeeee!! What happened to you?"

Faintly, I heard Eddie's answer. "Arp arp arp."

I pocketed his sugar cookies and left. He probably wouldn't feel much like eating them anyway.

The next day I rode over to Eddie's house to see if he could play. He was in bed in his pajamas, with bandages sticking out the legs and sleeves. One of his ankles was as big as a grapefruit—a spoiled grapefruit. Both his eyes were black and blue, and swelled shut, except for a narrow slit in one eye. I could see him peering at me out of that slit.

"I didn't cry, did I? If you say I did, you're lying."

"You didn't cry," I said. "A lot of guys would have cried, but you didn't. Any more than I would have."

Eddie leaned back on his pillows and smiled with satisfaction. "That was a terrific crash, wasn't it?"

"Yeah," I said. "The best I ever seen."

"Look at these eyes and my ankles. They're awful, ain't they?" He grinned. "Norm and Jackie and Kenny are all coming over this afternoon to look at me. Boy, I bet I almost make them sick."

"You almost make me sick," I said.

"Really? You're not just saying that? Hey, listen, I'm gonna get some terrific scabs out of this. When they get ready, you can come over and watch me peel 'em off. Okay?"

"Yeah, sure," I said. "Well, I gotta go. See ya later, Eddie."

Pedaling my bike back home, I couldn't help but feel depressed. There was poor Eddie in bed, all stung and sprained and cut and bruised and scraped practically to pieces. I couldn't understand why it had happened to him, my best friend. Some guys had all the luck.

Real Ponies Don't Go Oink!

EVEN WHEN WE WERE SMALL boys, Crazy Eddie Muldoon and I were gnawed by that terrible hunger known to nearly every boy in that distant time, the hunger for our very own pony to ride. We dreamed the impossible dream: on our next birthday, or surely the one after, we would awaken to hear our beaming parents gush, "Guess what's tied up out behind the woodshed, Son. But before you rush off to see what it is, you'd better open this present that's in the shape of a saddle." Sure enough, the present would be a saddle! Then you would tear out of the house and there, hidden behind the woodshed, probably with a big bow around its neck, would be your . . . very . . . own . . . pony! You would saddle up your pony and gallop off toward the horizon, pausing only long enough to wave to your generous and thoughtful and loving parents, the very best parents in the whole world.

My family wasn't big on impossible dreams. "Would you shut up about a pony!" my mother roared every time I brought up the topic. "Ponies cost money! You think money grows on trees?"

Occasionally, I would ride one of our pigs by the kitchen window, hoping to shame Mom into buying me a pony. "There goes old short-in-the-saddle," my sister, the Troll, would shout. "Hopalong Hog and Gene Oink, the smelly cowboy!" Then she and Mom would have a good laugh. Their response didn't leave me much hope of ever getting my very own pony by appealing to sympathy.

Crazy Eddie fared scarcely better. "Would you shut up about a pony!" Mr. Muldoon would roar. "Ponies cost money! You think money grows on trees?" Still, the Muldoons had an actual farm, with cows, sheep, pigs, chickens, rabbits, and even a goat, which, by the way, wasn't a bad ride. A pony would have fit right in to the Muldoon menagerie. If you stared hard enough at their pasture, you could easily imagine a pony out there. You could almost see it in fact, and one morning I *did* see it! Galloping majestically across the pasture was—forget the dumb pony—a beautiful, huge, glistening black horse!

Eddie was riding the horse.

It was almost too much for me to bear. True, Eddie didn't exactly fit my idea of a cowboy. The horse's back was so broad that Eddie's stubby legs stuck straight out on either side, as if he were doing an equestrian version of the splits. Eddie and the horse were totally out of aesthetic proportion to each other. From a distance, the two of them looked like a mouse riding a tall dog, although I knew the image would hurt Eddie's feelings.

"You look like a mouse riding a tall dog!" I called out to him.

Eddie galloped over, reined in right next to me, and glared down. He had to lean out precariously in order to see over the curve of the horse's barrel-shaped belly. "You're just jealous," Eddie said. "I bet you want a ride."

"Naw," I said. "I'm expecting my own pony any day now. I'll wait and ride it."

"If you climb up the barbwire and stand on top of that fence post, I'll pull you up," Eddie said.

"Okay," I said.

I climbed the post and Eddie hauled me up behind him. The view was wonderful from up there. You could see practically forever. The two of us rode off singing "Back in the Saddle Again," even though this was only our first time in the saddle. Our legs jutted straight out to the side, so there was no reason to argue about who got to use the stirrups. Actually, doing the splits while trotting about on horseback isn't nearly as painful as it sounds. Excruciating, yes, but scarcely more uncomfortable than that. Cowboys are tough.

It turned out that Old Tom, the horse, had recently been destined for another existence in the form of fox food. One of the farmers up the road raised foxes for their furs, and many a worn-out horse ended up there as the luncheon special. Apparently, the farmer had an excess of fox food for the moment and asked Eddie's father if he had use for a horse. Mr. Muldoon said he could probably think of one, if he put his mind to it.

Old Tom had already done a little time at the fox farm and, while exhausting the appeals process, had got religion. He had been a bad horse, even a wicked horse, and his former owner had finally got fed up with his behavior and sent him up the road. His first week at the Muldoons, Tom was still figuratively wiping the sweat from his brow over his narrow escape from a career as fox food. You couldn't have asked for a sweeter, gentler horse for two little boys.

After a week or two, however, Old Tom apparently forgot his last-minute reprieve. He got it into his head that he had always lived at the Muldoon farm and, furthermore, probably owned it. He soon relapsed to his former nasty self. Hardly a day went by that he didn't buck us off. While we tried to get his bridle on he would casually place a hoof on one of my feet. Then he would put all his weight on that one hoof, balancing there, with daylight showing between the ground and his other three hooves. I would be yelling and thrashing about, and Tom would nonchalantly turn his head and look back, as if wondering what all the ruckus was about. Eddie would be trying to get the bridle over Tom's ears, and the horse would suddenly jerk his head up and send Eddie flying. Old Tom was wearing us out. He finally became so haughty he decided he didn't want to be ridden at all. Practically every day, carrying his bridle, we trailed Tom from one end of the farm to the other and back again, but almost never caught him. Then Eddie came up with the idea of roping the horse when it came to get a drink from the watering trough. First, though, we needed to find a rope.

Eddie's father had been putting a new layer of shingles on the barn and had bought a long rope that he tied to a big thick belt around his waist. He fastened the other end of the rope to a tractor, then climbed up a ladder and worked his way up over the steep roof of the barn to the far side, where the rope held him in place while he worked on the shingles. We found the rope neatly coiled by the tractor with the belt resting on top of the coil. Mr. Muldoon must have been taking a coffee break in the house, because he was nowhere in sight. Eddie looked this way and that, and then said he didn't think his pa would mind our using the rope to lasso Old Tom.

"I wish Pa was a cowboy or rancher, instead of just a farmer," Eddie said, grunting as he hoisted the big coil of rope and draped it over his shoulder. "Or a professional baseball player. That would be good. But he's just so ordinary. All he does is dumb things, like put new shingles on the barn. It's sort of embarrassing."

"Yeah," I said, trying to sound sympathetic, as though my family were interesting.

I suggested to Eddie that we cut off a piece of rope long enough for a lariat, but Eddie said no, it might make his pa mad. He said it would be better if we used the whole rope and just tied a loop in one end. He hauled all the rope out to the watering trough, tied a loop, and climbed up on the corral fence above the trough. The excess rope was scattered about the barnyard behind us in coils and assorted snarls.

Presently, Tom came moseying out of the pasture and headed for the trough. He stopped and eyed us suspiciously. Satisfied that he could handle anything we might have thought up for him, he plodded on in.

"What are you boys up to now?" growled Mr. Muldoon, coming behind us. Startled, we both jumped.

"Nothin' Pa," Eddie said. "Why?"

"Why! Well, because you got my new safety rope snarled all over the barnyard, that's why!"

"Sorry, Pa," Eddie said, turning his attention back to Tom. The horse was dipping its muzzle into the trough. "We're just trying to catch Old Tom."

"He's a lazy beast," Mr. Muldoon said. Both Eddie and I were intently watching Old Tom. It was only much later that we learned Mr. Muldoon had picked up his safety belt and strapped it on. "I'd help you catch him, Son, but I got to get this barn shingled before it starts to rain."

"That's okay, Pa," Eddie said. "I think we just about got him."

Mr. Muldoon started untangling the safety rope and forming it into a coil on the ground.

Tom lifted his dripping muzzle from the trough and glared up at us, his ears flattened back against his head. Eddie tossed the lasso around his neck and jerked it tight.

The horse reared up, pawed the air, and whinnied angrily. Then it bolted for the pasture. The rope sizzled through Eddie's hands. "Ow!" he cried, jerking away. "That burns!"

"Now what's got into Old Tom?" Mr. Muldoon said, looking up from his coil of rope. "Stupid horse!"

"I lassoed him," Eddie explained.

"You did?" Mr. Muldoon said. "With wha—?"

All the loops and turns and tangles of rope slithered this way and that and then snapped straight out toward the pasture. The coil at Mr. Muldoon's feet disappeared like a giant strand of spaghetti slurped from a plate. At that instant Mr. Muldoon took the longest step I'd ever seen anyone take in my life. He must have stepped a good thirty feet from takeoff to touchdown. Both Eddie and I were impressed.

"Wow!" Eddie cried. "Did you see that! Holy smokes! And look at Pa go now! I never knew he could run so fast! He must be trying to help us catch old Tom!"

He sounded so pleased and proud that I couldn't help but envy him. Eddie obviously had the fastest father in the county, maybe in the whole country or even the world.

Old Tom must have been surprised, too, and

even terrified, when he saw Mr. Muldoon racing after him at such amazing speed for a mere human. Tom kicked up his heels, stretched out, and ran even harder, as if his life depended on it, which, as we later learned, it did.

Eddie and I watched until his pa and Tom disappeared into the creek bottom, both of them practically flying. As far as we could judge, though, Mr. Muldoon wasn't gaining an inch on the horse.

"Shucks," Eddie said. "Pa ain't ever gonna catch Tom just by chasing him. He should know better. A horse can outrun a man every time, even one as fast as Pa."

"Hard to say," I said. "Your pa was really moving. I bet if he wasn't wearing his big ol' clodhopper boots he could."

"Maybe," Eddie said. "But there's no point in us waiting around for them to get back. We might as well go do something else. Got any ideas?"

"We could go ride your pigs," I said. "To tell you the truth, I'm kinda sick of horses."

"Yeah, me too," Eddie said. "So which pig you want to ride, Trigger or Champ?"

7
Secret Places

ALL MY LIFE I have had secret places. I like secret places. They make me feel smug and superior, two of the really great feelings.

"I've got this secret place," you tell a friend. Right away he wants to know where it is. "I can't tell you," you say, smugly, superiorly. "It's a secret."

I also hate secret places—other people's. Ross Russell has a secret hunting place I've been trying to pry out of him for years.

"C'mon, Ross, you can tell me," I say. "I won't ever sneak up there to hunt without you. We've been friends for forty years. What are friends for, if not to tell their secret hunting places? Just tell me, okay?"

"Can't. It's a secret."

"Tell me your secret hunting place if you want to live!"

I have about three dozen secret places scattered around the country. Some are nothing more than small, gravelly beaches; others are entire mountain valleys and even mountain ranges. Often, I come across other people in my secret places. They, of course, have just as much right to be there as I do. It's very irritating.

I suppose it's all right to share your secret places with strangers, as long as you don't have to share the secret.

When I was a boy, I loved secret places even more than I do now. Within a three-mile radius of our farm, I had staked out hundreds of secret places—fishing holes, hunting spots, caves, swamps, lookout trees, old cabins, and even several culverts under the highway. Some of my secret spots were shared with particular friends.

"This will be our secret spot," I would say to my friend. "Nobody else will know about it."

"Okay," he would say. Then we would take a spit oath. If I had taken a blood oath for every one of my secret spots I shared with someone, I would have been a quart low most of the time. Besides, spit oaths are much less painful than blood oaths. Occasionally, I would fall off a cow or a pig or something and end up with a bloody nose. That was the only time I cared about taking a blood oath.

"Let's say this is our secret spot and take a blood

oath on it," I'd tell Crazy Eddie Muldoon as I tried to dam the flow of blood from a nostril.

"In the middle of a cow pasture?" he'd say. "This isn't a good secret place."

"It's good enough," I'd reply. "I want to take a blood oath on it. So cut your finger."

"I don't want to cut my finger, not for a blood oath on a secret place in the middle of a lousy cow pasture. Why don't we both just use your blood?"

"Okay." Eddie had the right instincts.

Secret spots seldom had any special use other than to be secret. Fishing holes made good secret spots and were useful, but mostly what we did in secret spots was to sit around in them feeling smug and superior. It was quite evident to us that half the population of the world was simply dying to know the location of our secret spot, and that was sufficient for us.

Crazy Eddie and I did find one secret spot that we put to excellent use. One day we crawled up to the naked joists in the Muldoon garage. There were a few boards scattered around on the joists to walk on, so we walked on them, holding our arms out like tightrope walkers to maintain our balance and keep from smashing our skulls on the concrete floor below. We came to a sheet of plywood laid over the joists like an island in the air and stopped there to rest. There were some boxes stacked on the sheet of plywood and we sat down on them.

"Hey, you know what, Eddie," I said. "This would make a great secret place for us."

"Yeah," he said. "Good idea. We can come up here and . . . and . . . well, we can come up here."

"Sure," I said. "This would be perfect for that. Hey, what's in the boxes?"

Eddie lifted a lid. "Just some empty canning jars."

"Maybe we can think of something to do with them."

Eddie smiled. "I got an idea. We could fill them."

"Fill them with what?"

Eddie explained what we could fill them with.

"Hey, that's good," I said. "It will be kind of like scientific research. We can see how long it takes us to fill all these jars." Eddie and I started our research immediately, and managed to fill one of the jars about one-third full, which wasn't bad, considering we were acting on short notice. We screwed the lid back on the jar and set it neatly back in its box. Scientific research was fun.

The project was started in late spring. We worked on it well into the hot days of summer. Our dedication was enormous. A group of us kids would be fishing off the Sand Creek bridge, and Eddie would say, "Oh oh, I've got to go to the bathroom." Then he would leap on his bicycle and ride madly off toward the secret place in his garage, where I knew he would climb the ladder, balance his way across the boards on the ceiling joists to the sheet of plywood, and make a contribution to the scientific project.

The other kids would stare after Eddie as he pedaled frantically off up Sand Creek Hill. "How come Eddie rides his bike all the way home to go to the bathroom?" someone would ask me, this not being the standard practice of the group.

"Can't tell you," I'd say. "Eddie and I are conducting a secret scientific experiment in our secret place."

"C'mon, tell us!"

"Nope. Can't. It's a secret." I'd feel smug and superior all over.

One sizzling hot July day, I asked Eddie what the count was now.

"Thirty-nine full and a good start on the fortieth. But we're almost out of jars."

"Maybe you could ask your mom for some more empty jars," I suggested.

"Maybe."

We headed for Eddie's house to ask his mom for some more empty jars. As we were passing the open door of the Muldoon garage, we noticed Mr. Muldoon's legs disappearing up a ladder in the direction of our secret place. Pretty soon we could hear him tramping across the narrow board walkway on the ceiling joists.

"What are you doing up there, Pa?" Eddie called out nervously. Obviously, Mr. Muldoon had no idea he was violating a secret place.

"Oh, I stored a couple of planks up here. Stay where you are. I may need some help getting them down." He stepped onto the plywood sheet that formed the floor to our secret place. "Now what's this. Well, I'll be dang. Your ma's got some kind of canned goods stored up here. Why would she put it up here instead of in the cellar? Looks like some kind of juice. I don't know what's got into that woman. This stuff's probably spoiled, simmering up here in this heat. I better open a jar and see what it is."

Eddie and I looked at each other. He could tell I was winding up my mainspring that would shoot me off home. "Pa," he said, "I don't think you should—"

We heard the tinny *plink* of a lid popping off a canning jar, followed by a strangled, choking shout from Mr. Muldoon. We could hear him staggering about, then crashing into the crate of jars. The jars tumbled down onto the concrete floor in a series of magnificent golden explosions. Powerful toxic fumes filled the garage, bringing tears to our eyes. "*Aaaack*!" cried Mr. Muldoon, who apparently thought he, too, was being destroyed. We watched in horror as he leaped about in a series of pirouettes on the naked joists above, until at last he dropped into a space between them, luckily catching himself by the armpits. He then hung by his hands and dropped to the floor, apparently spraining both ankles, or so I judged from the manner in which he came hobbling out of the clouds of fumes, choking and gasping.

"Pa! Pa!" shouted Eddie. "You destroyed our experiment! A whole summer's work!"

A rare moment of insight into the peculiar workings of Mr. Muldoon's mind told me that the destruction of our summer's work was the least of our concerns. "Got to go home," I said to Eddie.

"Oh, okay," he said. "See you later."

As I released my mainspring and shot by Mr. Muldoon, who was hunched over choking and coughing and wiping his streaming nose and eyes, I very much doubted whether Eddie had a later.

One of the best things you can do with a secret place is share it with a special friend. Sometimes, though, you don't even like the person you choose to share a secret place with. It is one of those strange psychological aberrations beyond human comprehension.

My father died when I was six. Five years later, my mother remarried. I did not much care for my new stepfather at first. The only good thing about Hank was that he liked to fish, even though he wasn't very good at it. From time to time, he would take me fishing and try to make amends for rudely invading my domain, but I wasn't having any of it. We almost never caught any fish anyway.

Hank was so poor at fishing he was ecstatic whenever he caught so much as a little seven-inch trout, and he would even tell the neighbors about this fish he had caught. It was embarrassing. I hated to go places with him, it was so embarrassing to hear him tell his fish stories. He didn't even know how to lie properly: he would go into all the details about how he had baited his hook and dropped it into the current just so and let it drift down behind a sunken stump, and then describe the thrilling strike of the fish.

"Gosh, how big was that fish, Hank?" the neighbor would ask.

Lie, Hank! I'd plead silently. *Lie!*

"Oh, a good seven inches," Hank would say truthfully.

"Umm," the neighbor would politely respond.

Stream fishing opened the first week of June. Huge cutthroat trout continued their spawning run up Sand Creek for exactly a week after the opening. One day the cutthroats would be there, and the next they would be gone. Hank knew nothing about the run of big trout. When opening day arrived, he was prepared to go out after another seven-incher. It was bad enough that I had to put up with a new stepfather. I simply couldn't stand the further embarrassment of listening to him tell his small-fish stories, particularly to fishermen who would have spent the day hauling out huge cutthroat.

Before first light on opening day, Hank and I headed down to Sand Creek. Practically the entire town had emptied out and now lined the banks of the creek to have a go at the cutthroat. Hank, of course, thought everybody was after his seven-incher.

"Cripes," he said. "I think I'll go back home. We'd have to stand in line to get a chance to cast into the crick." Because Hank had never seen anybody else fish Sand Creek, he probably had come to think of it as his own secret place. He seemed depressed. Here he'd had his heart set on catching his seven-incher on opening day and now it was ruined for him.

"Good idea, Hank," I said. "You better go home."

He turned and started to walk back to the house.

At that moment I was overcome by one of those weaknesses of character I despise so much in myself. "Wait," I said. "Wait, Hank. I'll take you to my secret place."

"Secret place?" he said. "What secret place?"

There was a large bend in Sand Creek that no one ever fished because the brush was so high and thick that it was assumed to be impassable. It was further assumed that if a person managed to fight his way through the brush, there would be no place to stand to fish the creek. But a couple of days before opening, I had found that I could crawl through the brush on my hands and knees. And on the other side of the brush, I discovered a tiny gravel beach right upstream from a magnificent fishing hole! It was one of the finest secret places I've ever come across.

Half an hour later, Hank and I were crawling through the brush on our hands and knees. I let Hank go first to break trail. With typical clumsiness, he let a branch snap back and hit me in the nose. I could feel the trickle of blood begin to flow. The man was hopeless.

His first five casts, Hank caught five cutthroat all upward of two pounds, one approaching five. He was practically shedding his skin from the pure joy of it. "I can't believe it!" he cried. "This is wonderful! I never realized fish this big even existed!" His eyes were disgustingly moist.

Still dabbing at my bloody nose, I had not yet got a line in the water. Hank hadn't even waited for me to get ready, he was such a fish hog.

"You know what, Pat," he shouted at me. "From now on, this will be our secret place! Just yours and mine!"

"Oh yeah?" I said. "In that case, cut your finger."

"How come?"

"'Cause we have to take a blood oath on a secret place. Don't you know that?"

Hank stared at me, as his shaking hands unhooked a twenty-inch cutthroat. "Maybe we could both just use your blood," he said. "How does that sound?"

It sounded all right to me. I figured Hank might not turn out too badly after all, with the proper amount of training. He seemed to have the right instincts.

A Really Nice Blizzard

HENRY P. GROGAN, proprietor of Grogan's War Surplus, glanced up from his cash register as Crazy Eddie Muldoon and I bolted through the front door of his establishment.

"Quick, Mr. Grogan," Crazy Eddie shouted, "we need to buy a parachute!"

"A parachute? What you boys need a parachute for? And why ain't you in school? You fellas playin' hooky?"

"No, we're not playing hooky," I said. "They let us out early when the blizzard got too dangerous for us kids to stay at school. We've got to hurry because the school bus leaves to take us home in fifteen minutes."

"I don't know about sellin' a parachute to two

fool kids," Grogan said. "You probably got some notion about jumpin' off a barn roof with it, ain'tcha? Gitcher selves killed or worse doin' something like that. No, I wouldn't feel right about it."

"We got over seven dollars between us," Crazy Eddie said, looking the proprietor right in the eye.

"But I've been wrong, before," Grogan said. "Lemme see your money."

That was one of the things I liked about Crazy Eddie and Mr. Grogan. They both knew how to do a deal.

As Eddie and I hurried toward the door with our parachute, Grogan called after us. "Just out of idle curiosity, boys, what *are* you gonna do with that parachute?"

"Oh," I said, "because we got out of school on account of the blizzard, Eddie and I thought we could rig a sail with the parachute on a sled and sail across a field. This is the only good blizzard we might get this year, and we don't want to waste it."

"Sounds reasonable to me," Grogan said. "I always did like a good blizzard myself."

When we got home and tried to hook up the sail to my sled, we discovered that rigging a mast with an old two-by-four and a broom handle wasn't easy. We struggled with the contraption until we were both half frozen. Finally I said, "We'd better go get

Rancid to help us. He'll know how to hook up a sail. Rancid knows just about everything."

Crazy Eddie and I tramped through the blizzard to Rancid's shack and, covered with a snow veneer, burst in without bothering to knock. The old woodsman was standing by his barrel stove, stirring something in a frying pan with a hunting knife. He leaped back with the knife raised in a stabbing position, and yelled, "Aiiigh! Aiiigh!" (Later he told us that yelling "Aiiigh! Aiiigh!" in a shrill voice is a good way to confuse evil forest spirits until you can think of a good way to deal with them.)

"Gol-dang an' tarnation, ain't you fellas ever heard about knockin'? Why, in another second Ah mighta had both of you chopped up into itty-bitty pieces! Ah got lightnin' relaxes."

Eddie and I shook off our coating of snow onto Rancid's floor and rushed over to warm our hands by his stove.

"Why cain't the two of you shake off thet snow outdoors? Now it'll just melt and turn to mud. Ah'll be slippin' and slidin' on it all day. You raised in a barn?"

"Sorry," I said. "We were just about frozen. Anyway, what we want is to have you help us build something we can use to sail on the snow. We've got a parachute for the sail. It'll work great in this blizzard."

"Hmmmm," Rancid said. "Let me thank about it a spell. You boys want somethin' to eat? Ah got plenty to go around."

"I don't think . . ." I said.

"Sure," Crazy Eddie said. "I'm starved." He had never yet had the experience of eating with Rancid.

Rancid blew the dust off a couple of tin plates he kept for guests and scraped out a glob for each of us from the skillet. He ate his share out of the skillet with the hunting knife.

"This is pretty good, Mr. Crabtree," Eddie said. "What is it?"

"As best Ah can recall, it's some chopped up b'ar meat, b'iled taters, beans, a chunk of hog fat, and, uh, let's see, oh, some dried wild mushrooms and a couple of squirrels. Why, you thank your momma might want the recipe?"

"She might," Eddie said. "She wouldn't use the wild mushrooms, though, because she can't tell the difference between the good ones and the poison ones." He chuckled, presumably at his mother's ignorance of wild mushrooms.

Rancid joined him in the chuckle. "Thet's okay, Ah cain't tell them apart neither."

"You *can't*?" Eddie croaked, staring down at the few little bites left on his plate.

"Nope, Ah cain't. But don't you worry none. Ah always tests wild mushrooms out on maw dog, Sport. If he likes 'em and don't drop daid, Ah eats 'em mawsef. Fed him a batch of these mushrooms a couple hours ago. Here, Sport, come show Eddie here you ain't daid. Sport! Here, Sport! Sport! Where is thet dang dog? He always comes when Ah calls him."

Eddie rose slowly from his chair, wild-eyed and suddenly pale. I stared uneasily at him as he selected a finger to put down his throat.

"Don't do it, Eddie," I said. "I'm still eating. Besides, Rancid doesn't have a dog."

After we'd all had a good laugh over the mushrooms and Rancid's mythical dog, Eddie and I presented our idea about the sailing parachute to the old woodsman.

"If thar's one thang Ah knows about, it's parachutes," he said authoritatively. "Ah done a lot of parachutin' in the Great War. General used to have me dropped behind enemy lines to do spyin' work. Ah ever tell you about the time—"

"Yeah," I said. "But what about using the parachute as a sail in the blizzard?"

"A sled won't work," Rancid said. "The sled will cut through the snow crust and you'll be stuck tighter'n a fly on a stirrin' spoon. You needs somethin' flat on the bottom, somethin' like a big pan."

"Shoot!" Eddie said. "There ain't no pan that big. Right now we've got this great blizzard and no way to use it!"

"Hold on a sec," Rancid said, putting on his thoughtful expression. "Hot dang, Ah thank Ah got just the thang!"

He stomped outside and soon returned with a large, curved metal object. He banged the snow off it onto the floor, in his enthusiasm apparently having forgotten about turning the floor to mud.

"What is it?" I asked.

"A fender off an old wrecked truck. Been keepin' it out in the yard. Figured some use would turn up fer it, and one has."

Eddie and I shouted with joy and relief. We would be able to put the blizzard to good use after all.

Rancid was a person who could never take a good idea and leave it alone. He had to improve on it. Eddie's plan had been for us to sail across the open fields on the icy crust burnished to a high polish by the wind and driven snow. Rancid, however, said the best idea would be to hike over to the Old Market Road. "It's just one long strip of shiny ice," he said. "It's so slick thar won't be nobody drivin' on it, thet's fer shore. We can have it all to ourselves."

"But what about a mast?" Eddie said.

"Won't need a mast," Rancid said. "Ah'll show you how it's done."

We cut through the woods to the Old Market Road, and sure enough, there was not a vehicle on it as far as we could see through the driven snow. Off in the distance, an undisturbed snowdrift slanted across the road. We had to lean into the wind in order to stand, and even then our feet skittered along on the snow-polished ice. It was slick.

Rancid threw the fender down with a metallic *ker-whump*. "Which one of you boys wants to go fust?"

"Let me try it," Crazy Eddie said.

Getting no argument from me, he climbed into the cavity of the upside-down fender and lay down on his belly.

"Thet ain't no way to do it," Rancid said. "Git up out of thar and let me show you how."

Rancid got in the fender, sitting upright. "Now hand me the parachute harness." For an old experienced parachuter, he didn't seem to know much about putting on the harness, but I suppose so much time had passed since the Great War that he had forgotten. Finally, he simply tied various straps of the harness around his waist and let it go at that. Then he grabbed a cluster of shroud lines in each hand like so many reins.

"Now here's the idear," he said. "Eddie, you take the bundle of parachute out in front. When Ah gives the signal, you throw the chute open so the wind can catch it. Pat, you push on the back of the fender to get me goin' so's the chute can pull me along. Ah'll show you how it's done. Then you fellas can give it a try."

Crazy Eddie and I, slipping and sliding on the icy roadway and fighting against the fierce wind, took up our assigned positions.

"Okay, ready?"

"Yeah!" Eddie and I yelled against the pounding wind.

"On the count of three!" Rancid yelled. "One! Two! ThreeEEEEEEEEEEEE . . . !"

Eddie and I skated along the road, driven by the wind at our backs. There was no sign of Rancid, except an occasional blasted-out snowdrift marked by a spray of tobacco juice and claw marks that looked as if they might have been made by human hands.

After a while we stopped at a farmhouse and knocked. A skinny old man in bib overalls and a flannel shirt opened the door and stared down at us.

"What in tarnation you boys doin' out in a storm like this? You look half froze. Come in by the fire and thaw out."

"Thanks," I said. "But we were lookin' for our

friend, Rancid Crabtree. He went by here on the road about half an hour ago."

The farmer scratched his jaw. "Nope, can't say I seen anybody go by. You're lookin' for Crabtree, you say. What was he drivin'?"

"An upside-down truck fender," Crazy Eddie said.

"Yes," I said. "And he was wearing a parachute and—"

"Oh, Mavis," the farmer called out to his wife. "Better put some hot chocolate on for these boys. I think the cold's about got 'em. How do you fellas feel, anyway?"

"I don't feel so good," Eddie said. "But I think it may have been some poison mushrooms I ate for lunch."

"I see," said the farmer. "Poison mushrooms. Hurry up with that hot chocolate, Mavis."

After the hot chocolate, and not knowing anything else to do, Eddie and I returned to Rancid's shack. Much to our relief, the old woodsman came in a short while later, looking like a tattered icicle in more or less human form. The cut ends of the parachute harness dangled from his snow-caked waist.

"You don't look too good, Mr. Crabtree," Crazy Eddie said with rare understatement.

Rancid sank down on a chair and dug some snow out of his whitened ears with a blue finger. "Oh yeah?" he snarled. "Wal, you wouldn't neither if you'd been blowed halfway 'cross the gol-dang county in a truck fender. Ah'd still be goin' iffen Ah hadn't had the good fortune to get snared by a barbwire fence and torn dang near to shreds and . . ."

As he ranted on, I heard a sad sound from outside. With one last thrust at tearing the shakes from the roof, the wind dropped away with a rattling moan. The blizzard was dying. It had been a fine blizzard, and I was sorry to see it pass away.

Cubs

I LIKE TO THINK I was just as good a Cub Scout as the next guy, the next guy being Grover Finch, who was about as miserable a Cub Scout as ever tied a granny knot and called it square.

Our den could boast of boys clearly cut out for the scouting life, but I wasn't one of them. Neither was Grover. He dropped out of Cubs shortly after the strange incident at Camp Muskrat. I think he may have received a dishonorable discharge, but I don't know for sure.

It was Grover who taught us a lot of good stuff not covered in the Cub Scout manual. He showed us how to tie a hangman's knot and also demonstrated how it worked, slipping the loop over Terry

Greer's head and pulling it tight. Terry got into the act and made a strangling noise, then flopped on his back on the floor of our den mother's living room, his tongue sticking out six inches and his eyeballs protruding comically. It was wonderfully realistic, particularly because his tongue was all purple from a grape sour ball.

Mrs. Slocum, our den mother, came in from the kitchen about that time carrying a tray of hot cocoa and cookies. Her eyes protruded even more than Terry's. Then Grover, never one to leave well enough alone, said, "Caught him stealin' cattle, ma'am, so we strung him up." Mrs. Slocum released a screech that sent her cat halfway to the ceiling and then out of the room without ever touching the floor. Displaying an athletic prowess we never suspected, our plump, matronly den mother bounded over a wing chair and a coffee table with the agility of a startled gazelle, dropped on poor terrified Terry with all fours, ripped the noose off over his head, and pumped down on his chest so hard that the sour ball shot three feet into the air.

As soon as we got Mrs. Slocum calmed down a bit, a couple of us pried her cat off the kitchen wall and gave it to her to pet, just to show we were trustworthy, loyal, and helpful. The only real damage was cocoa stains that never did come out of our Cub

Scout shirts. Cookies had sprayed the room like shrapnel, but they were the soft kind, and didn't hurt much. If they had been my grandmother's sugar cookies, somebody might have been decapitated.

Most of our Cub Scout meetings from then on were pleasant but uneventful. We practiced our other knots—the hangman's had been banned—and worked on various projects thought up by Grover. The most interesting of these was the snowball catapult, constructed in the den mother's backyard out of a two-by-four, a couple of bicycle-tire inner tubes, and various odds and ends. It was powerful. Mrs. Slocum thought it was some sort of teeter-totter, until it fired a ten-pound snowball across three backyards and nearly took out old Mr. Fuller, who was carrying an armload of firewood at the time. He thought he had been narrowly missed by a meteorite, which was fortunate for us. If he'd had any previous experience with ten-pound snowballs, we might have been in a lot of trouble.

More often than not, we didn't have time to work up an interesting project, because Mrs. Slocum came down with a "sick headache" almost every week, and we had to adjourn the meeting early. I remember how disappointed we were when one of Mrs. Slocum's sick headaches forced us to abort Terry's test flight, after we had worked so hard to make him a parachute, in case he experienced technical problems during reentry.

Grover became increasingly bored, and I expected him to go AWOL at any time. Then one day in early spring, the scoutmaster of the local troop showed up at our meeting. Mr. Tiddle was a robust outdoorsman, shaped something like a barrel, but all bone and muscle. He frequently hiked his scouts into the ground and then ran up and down a mountain a couple of times just to work up a sweat, a feat about which he didn't mind boasting. He lifted weights and did calisthenics just for the fun of it, but the strangest thing was that every New Year's Day he would chop a big hole in the ice and plunge into the frigid water of Lake Blight. He claimed the icy plunge was wonderfully invigorating and recommended it highly to the local townsfolk. A few said they might give it a try, if their present supply of misery ran low and they had to restock.

"Boys," Mr. Tiddle boomed to us at our meeting, "I've got great news for you. A couple of the scouts from Troop Nine-oh-seven and I are going to take you Cubs on an overnight outing to Camp Muskrat this Saturday. How does that sound?"

We broke into cheers, with Grover cheering the loudest of all.

"You all show up at the school at eight o'clock Saturday, and we'll issue you sleeping bags and packs," Mr. Tiddle said. He then went on to tell us what clothes, grub, and gear to bring. "For supper, we'll treat you to a wiener roast."

"Yayyyyyyyyy!"

"It's about time we got to see some action," Grover said.

The next Saturday morning, about fifteen of us Cubs assembled at the grade school. Several station wagons were parked nearby. We assumed they were there to transport us to Camp Muskrat, located on a small lake five miles from town. Then we noticed that volunteered fathers were loading the station wagons with tents and other gear and supplies. We watched as the station wagons departed one by one, until none were left for us. We exchanged uneasy glances. Surely it was not intended that our short puny legs hike all the way to Camp Muskrat.

Mr. Tiddle and two Boy Scouts, all three in their starched tan uniforms, strode briskly over to us. "Listen up, Cubs!" Mr. Tiddle bellowed in his most enthusiastic tone. "We have a real treat for you. Scouts Lucifer and Attila have volunteered to serve as your leaders on the campout, and they have come up with a marvelous idea. Instead of riding to Camp Muskrat, you get to practice your hiking skills all the way out to the camp. Let's have a big hand for these fine scouts."

Clap clap. We stared up at the towering scouts,

both of whom smiled benevolently down on us. "I leave you in their care," Mr. Tiddle said. "See you all at Camp Muskrat." He got into his car and drove away.

The two scouts watched his car until it disappeared around a corner. When they turned back to us, we were shocked. They had grown fangs and claws and their eyes glowed red with fiery light! We could tell from their gleefully evil expressions this was an opportunity they had waited for all their lives.

"Hoist your packs and line up according to height, shrimps!" Attila bellowed at us in a pretty good imitation of Mr. Tiddle, only mean and threatening. "No talking! Move it! Move it!"

Startled, we hoisted our packs and scrambled into a ragged line, ranging from four-foot Peewee Thompson at one end to five-foot Leonard Brisco at the other. The packs had been intended for actual scouts and were too big for most of us. Peewee looked like a pack with legs.

"Hey, I just remembered," Porky Singleton cried out. "I'm supposed to go to the dentist today! See you guys later."

"I have to go to the bathroom," Danny Murphy yelled. "Be right back."

"Me too," shouted Tony Naccarado. "Be gone just a second."

"Shut up, shrimps!" snarled Lucifer. "Back in formation!" The would-be deserters shrank back into line.

"Left face!" screamed Lucifer.

"Forwarrrrd! March!" bellowed Attila. "Hut two three four, hut . . ."

Attila brought up the rear, apparently for the purpose of harrying the stragglers and shooting the wounded. We marched out of town and along the highway in a line that unkind observers described as looking like dusty blue gunk oozing from an invisible tube.

"How much farther is it?" croaked Peewee.

"Four miles to go!" shouted Lucifer, striding along. "Now close up that line! Hut two three four . . ."

The hot spots of blisters began to glow inside our tennis shoes. Pack straps gnawed at our shoulders.

"This ain't a hike," Grover muttered to me. "It's a death march!"

"Somebody is going to pay for this," I muttered back.

"You said it," Grover snarled, shooting Lucifer a wicked look. "Bring any rope?"

"Shut up, you two!" screamed Lucifer. "Hut two three . . ."

Hours later we limped into Camp Muskrat and dropped to the frozen, snow-blotched ground. Some of the packs looked as if they had finished the march on their own, but from beneath each crawled a wretched little blue-clad creature, one of whom was Peewee. "How much farther?" he gasped.

The fathers had set up the tents and then vanished with the blinding speed common to fathers volunteered for Cub Scout outings. Mr. Tiddle and the two scouts were now left alone with fifteen exhausted but surly Cubs, who sprawled in ominous silence, sullenly watching Attila, Lucifer, and Mr. Tiddle jog about gathering wood for the evening campfire. The scouts and scoutmaster joked and laughed as if they hadn't a care in the world. The air, however, was heavy with suspense, dark with foreboding.

I crawled over to the remains of Grover and Peewee. "Come up with anything for Lucifer and Attila yet?" I asked Grover.

"I'm thinking. I'm thinking," Grover said. "Everything I come up with is either too kind or too complicated. We need something simple but mean. I suppose we could steal their clothes so they would have to run around naked in the cold and maybe catch pneumonia and suffer horribly for a long time and then die terrible agonizing deaths. But I'd like to come up with something mean."

"I like it," Peewee said.

"Me too," I said. "But how do we get them out of their clothes?"

"That's the problem."

The sun sank behind Muskrat Mountain, and a breeze wafted in off Muskrat Lake, chilled by rafts of sludgy ice still drifting about the surface. We put on sweaters and even coats and gathered around the fire that Lucifer and Attila had built into a small inferno. This was more like it.

"Are we camping yet?" Peewee asked.

"I think so," I said.

Suddenly, Mr. Tiddle erupted from his tent with a towel thrown over his shoulder. "Any of you Cubs like to join me for a dip in the lake? What, no takers? Har har! Grow hair on your chests, boys, grow hair on your chests!"

"Grow hair all over me," Grover muttered. The other Cubs expressed the opinion that they had all the hair they needed or wanted.

"How about you scouts?" Mr. Tiddle boomed at Lucifer and Attila. "Like to refresh yourselves with a dip before supper? There's a nice sandy beach down the shore a ways, and we don't even have to chop through the ice. Just shove it out of the way."

Lucifer and Attila shuddered. "Why, we'd sure like to, Mr. Tiddle. Sounds wonderful. But darn it all, we didn't bring our bathing trunks."

"Me neither," bellowed Mr. Tiddle. "Ever hear of skinny-dipping? C'mon, lads. Race you out to the floating dock!"

"Wow, okay then, Mr. Tiddle," whined Lucifer. "Attila and I'll be right there, as soon as we grab some towels. Hope we can find you in the dark." The two scouts slouched off.

We Cubs edged closer to the toasty campfire. "This is too good to be true," Grover said to me. At first I thought he was talking about the fire, but he wasn't. "Be back in a bit," he said, and slipped off into the shadows.

Scarcely had Grover vanished when the plot thickened. The headlights of a car illuminated the Camp Muskrat parking area for a moment, and soon Mrs. Slocum and another lady came picking their way down a trail to the campfire.

"Good evening, Cubs!" cried our den mother. "You look like you're having a wonderful time. I'm so glad! I think you all know my good friend Mrs. Teasdale. We thought we would join you for the wiener roast. Brought you a treat—marshmallows!"

"Yayyyyyy!"

We pulled up a log for the ladies to sit on next to the fire. "My goodness, the mosquitoes are bad, and so early in the year, too," said Mrs. Teasdale. "Hope you all brought plenty of mosquito dope. Oh, I don't see Mr. Tiddle."

"He's out swimming," one of the Cubs said.

"Oh, that man!" Mrs. Teasdale giggled. "He is simply too much."

Just then Grover emerged from the woods, slapping his way through a cloud of mosquitoes.

"Why, Grover, where have you been off to?" the den mother asked. "Not up to some mischief, are you?"

"Kind of personal, ma'am," Grover replied, trying his best to look embarrassed.

"Oh, I see. Excuse me, dear." The two ladies giggled in motherly fashion.

"Snatched only one set of clothes and a towel," Grover whispered to me. "Was all I could find in the dark. I could hear them splashing around not too far from shore and thought they might spot me. Slipped the clothes into their tent. But either Lucifer or Attila is going to be in for a big surprise!"

We sat around the fire telling ghost stories, but nothing compared to the horror that awaited us. Sooner than expected, Lucifer came rushing into the light of the fire.

"Wow," he said. "You guys are smarter than you look. That water is liquid ice. Just lucky I had the good sense to test it with my toe first. Toe's still numb. Man, if I'd jumped in that lake I'd have froze my—why, hello there, Mrs. Slocum, Mrs. Teasdale. Didn't know you were coming for a visit."

"Attila's the one," Grover whispered to me, snickering behind his hand. "This could be good."

A minute later, Attila bounded into camp—fully clothed! "Wheweee, that water's cold! Chickening out is the better part of valor, I always say. I don't know how Mr. Tiddle can stand it."

Grover stared grimly at Lucifer and Attila.

Minutes dragged by. We sang a camp song. Mrs. Slocum and Mrs. Teasdale told about when they were little girls and had picked huckleberries in the hills above Camp Muskrat. Terry started to tell another ghost story, and then . . .

The monster roared out of the darkness so suddenly that several Cubs almost inhaled flaming marshmallows. For a moment I thought it was a Sasquatch, but it turned out to be Mr. Tiddle. He was stark naked, except for a little cedar bough he had twisted off a tree as a concession to modesty and our tender sensibilities. He probably could have done without the cedar bough, because he wore a layer of mosquitoes thick enough to serve as a fur coat.

"So, the old steal-the-clothes trick!" Mr. Tiddle boomed.

"I thought this might happen," Grover whispered. "You can have my bike and baseball glove if you want them."

"Thanks, Grover," I said. "Hey, it's been fun knowing you."

Then a surprising thing happened. Mr. Tiddle grabbed Lucifer and Attila by the hair, one with each hand. "Ha! Just as I suspected—hair's not even wet! Well, I'll just have to see what I can do about that."

"Wait!" croaked Attila.

"It wasn't . . . !" blurted Lucifer

"Oh, it wasn't, was it?" said Mr. Tiddle. "Well, we'll just check your tent and see if we don't find my clothes there."

"Good idea!" yelped Lucifer.

"You bet!" said Attila. "Check our tent!"

Mr. Tiddle dragged the two scouts over to check their tent.

"See," Lucifer said. "Your clothes aren't . . . *NOOOOOO*!"

"Aha!" cried Mr. Tiddle. "You two scalawags thought you could pull a fast one on me, did you?"

He snatched up each of the scouts by the back of the belt and charged off toward the lake, one in each meaty hand. The screams were among the best and most satisfying I've ever heard, starting low and quavering but then rising in pitch and volume while still conveying great feeling and intensity right up to the moment of total immersion. I thought I even heard one warbly scream from underwater, but it might have been a loon. We Cubs all agreed the performance was highly entertaining, spiritually enriching, and well worth a forced march.

Recovering his little cedar branch, Mr. Tiddle strolled back to the fire chortling. "Please excuse my nudity for a minute, boys. I just wanted to make a point about practical jokes—oh, nice to see you, Mrs. Slocum, Mrs. Teasdale. Didn't expect you ladies out this evening. The point I was making to the Cubs here is that people can play their little pranks, but in the end they have to pay the pipe—*Ladies*?" His lips froze in a grotesque smile over his big white teeth. He hunched over and tried to conceal himself behind the little bough. "Oh!"

I thought for a moment that Mr. Tiddle had blurted out a bad word, but then I realized a scoutmaster would never use a word like that. It was probably just the cry of some wild creature passing in the night.

Peewee said later that he thought it was all pretty funny, but that he couldn't help but feel sorry for Mr. Tiddle.

"I know what you mean," I said. "I sure would have felt embarrassed if I'd been standing there naked except for a little cedar bough and suddenly realized two ladies were sitting not ten feet away."

"Yeah," Peewee said. "Then, as if that wasn't bad enough, dumb ol' Terry accidentally flicks his flaming marshmallow onto the cedar bough. That ol' bough must have been dry as gunpowder, to flare up like that. Poor Mr. Tiddle."

"I think both Mrs. Slocum and Mrs. Teasdale handled it pretty well," I said. "It was nice how they pretended not to notice Mr. Tiddle because of concentrating so hard on twirling their sticks over the coals, just as if roasting wieners was the most important thing in the world to them."

"It would have been better if they hadn't let their wieners burn off and fall in the fire, though," Peewee said. "They didn't even seem to notice. Just sat there twirling them empty sticks round and round, and all the while Mr. Tiddle's roaring and darting about like a madman."

"Well, I guess that's camping," I said.

Grover never again showed up for a Cub Scout meeting. I guess he figured the campout at Muskrat Lake was the high point of scouting for him, and from then on it would be all downhill.

10

Muldoon in Love

AFTERWARDS, I FELT BAD for a while about Miss Deets, but Mom told me to stop fretting about it. She said the problem was Miss Deets had just been too delicate to teach third grade in our part of the country.

Besides being delicate, Miss Deets must have also been rich. I don't recall ever seeing her wear the same dress two days in a row. To mention the other extreme, Mr. Craw, one of the seventh-grade teachers at Delmore Blight Grade School, wore the same suit every day for thirty years. Once, when Mr. Craw was sick, the suit came to school by itself and taught his classes, but only Skip Moseby noticed that Mr. Craw wasn't inside the suit. Skip said the suit did a fair job of explaining dangling participles, which turned out to be a kind of South American lizard. I would have liked to hear the suit's lecture, because at the time I was particularly interested in lizards. But I digress from Miss Deets.

No one could understand why a rich and genteel lady like Miss Deets would want to teach third grade at Delmore Blight, but on the first day of school, there she was, smelling of perfume and money, her auburn hair piled on top of her head, her spectacles hanging by a cord around her long, slender, delicate neck. We stood there gawking at her, scarcely believing our good fortune in getting this beautiful lady as our very own third-grade teacher.

We boys all fell instantly in love with Miss Deets, but none more than my best friend, Crazy Eddie Muldoon. I loved her quite a bit myself at first, but Eddie would volunteer to skip recess so he could clean the blackboard erasers, whether they needed cleaning or not. For the first month of school, the third grade must have had the cleanest blackboard erasers in the entire history of Delmore Blight Grade School. For me, love was one thing, recess another. God had not intended the two to interfere with each other. But Crazy Eddie now skipped almost every recess in order to help Miss Deets with little chores around the classroom. She was depriving me of my best friend's company, and bit by bit I began to hate her. I wished Miss Deets would go away and never come back.

Worse yet, in his continuing efforts to prove his love for Miss Deets, Eddie started studying. He soon became the champion of our weekly spelling bees. "Wonderful, Edward!" Miss Deets would exclaim, when Eddie correctly spelled some stupid word nobody in the entire class would ever have reason to use. Then she would pin a ridiculous little paper star on the front of his shirt, the reward for being the last person standing in the spelling bee. It disgusted me to think Eddie would do all that work, learning how to spell all those words, for nothing more than having Miss Deets pin a ridiculous little paper star on his shirt.

Then one day Miss Deets made her fateful error. "Now, pupils," she announced, "I think it important for all young ladies and gentlemen to be able to speak in front of groups. So for the next few weeks we are going to have Show and Tell. Each day, one of you will bring one of your more interesting possessions to school, show it to the class, and then tell us all about it. Doesn't that sound like fun?"

Three-fourths of the class, including myself, cringed in horror. We didn't own *any* possessions, let alone interesting ones! Miss Deets looked at me and smiled. "Patrick, would you like to be first?"

I put on my thoughtful expression, as though mentally sorting through all my fascinating possessions to select just the one with which to enthrall the class. My insides, though, churned in terror and embarrassment. What could I possibly bring to Show and Tell? The only thing that came to mind was the family post-hole digger. I imagined myself standing up in front of the class and saying, "This is my post-hole digger. I dig post holes with it." No, Miss Deets probably had a longer speech in mind. I glanced around the room. Several hands of the rich kids from town were waving frantically for attention.

"Uh, I need more time," I told Miss Deets. Like about fifteen years, I thought, but I didn't tell her that.

"All right, then, Lester?" Miss Deets said to one of the rich kids. "You may be first."

The next day Lester brought his stamp collection to Show and Tell, and held forth on it for about an hour. An enterprising person could have cut the tedium into blocks and sold it for ice. But Miss Deets didn't seem to notice. "That's wonderful, Lester!" she cried. "Oh, I do think stamp collecting is such a rewarding hobby! Thank you very much, Lester, for such a fine and educational presentation. Would you like to clean the blackboard erasers during recess?"

I glanced at Crazy Eddie. He was yawning. Eddie had a habit of yawning to conceal his occasional moments of maniacal rage. Good, I thought.

At recess, Eddie refused to play. He stood with his hands jammed in his pockets, watching Lester on the third-grade fire escape, smugly pounding the blackboard erasers together. "Did you ever see anything more boring than that stupid stamp collection of Lester's?" he said to me.

"I think I did once," I said. "But it was so boring I forget what it was."

"I've got to come up with something for Show and Tell, something really good," Eddie said. "What do you think about a post-hole digger?"

Lester's stamp collection, however, was merely the beginning of a competition that was to escalate daily as each succeeding rich kid tried to top the one before. There were coin collections, doll collections, baseball-card collections, model airplanes powered by their own little engines, electric trains that could chew your heart out just looking at them, and on and on until we had exhausted the supply of rich kids in class. We were now down to us country kids, among whom there were no volunteers for Show and Tell. Miss Deets thought we were merely shy. She didn't realize we had nothing to show and tell about.

Rudy Griddle, ordered by Miss Deets to be the first of us to make a presentation, shuffled to the front of the class, his violent shaking surrounding him with a mist of cold sweat. He opened a battered cigar box and tilted it up so we could see the contents. "This here's my collection of cigarette butts," he said. "I pick 'em up along the road. You'll notice there ain't any shorter than an inch. If they's an inch or longer they's keepers. Some folks pick up cigarette butts to smoke, but I don't. I just collect them for educational purposes. Thank you." He returned to his desk and sat down.

The class turned to look at Miss Deets. Her mouth was twisted in revulsion. Suddenly, someone started clapping! Crazy Eddie Muldoon was applauding! And somebody else called out, "Yay, good job, Rudy!" The rest of us country kids joined in the applause and cheering and gave Rudy a standing ovation. He deserved it. After all, he had shown us the way. From now on, Show and Tell would *really* be interesting.

Farley Karp brought in the skunk hide he had tanned himself and gave a very interesting talk on the process, even admitting that he had made a few mistakes, but after all, it was the first skunk hide he had ever tanned. He said he figured from what he had learned on the first one, the next skunk hide he tanned he probably could cut the smell by a good 50 percent, which would be considerable.

Bill Stanton brought in his collection of dried wildlife droppings, which he had glued to a pine board in a tasteful display and varnished. It was a fine collection, with each item labeled as to its source.

Manny Fogg, who had been unable to think of a single thing to bring to Show and Tell, was fortunate enough to cut his foot with a double-bitted ax three days before his presentation and was able to come in and unwrap the bandages and show us the wound, which his mother had sewed shut with gut leader. It was totally ghastly but also very interesting, and educational too, particularly if you chopped firewood with a double-bitted ax, as most of us did.

Show and Tell had begun to tell on Miss Deets. Her face took on a wan and haunted look, and she became cross and jumpy. Once I think she went into the cloakroom and cried, because when she returned, her eyes were all red and glassy. That was the time Laura Ann Struddel brought in the chicken that all the other Struddel chickens had pecked half the feathers off of. Laura Ann had set the chicken on Miss Deets's desk and was using a pointer to explain the phenomenon. The chicken, looking pleased to be on leave from the other chickens, but also a little excited at being the subject of Show and Tell, committed a small indiscretion right there on Miss Deets's desk.

"Oh, my gahhh . . ." Miss Deets gasped, her face going as red as dewberry wine, while we third-graders had a good laugh. This, after all, was the first humor introduced into Show and Tell. From then on, those of us who still had to do Show and Tell tried to work a little comedy into our presentations, but nobody topped the chicken.

So many great things had been brought to Show and Tell by the other country kids that I had become desperate to find something of equal interest. Finally, I went with my road-killed toad, explaining how it had been flattened by a truck and afterwards had dried on the pavement, until I came along and peeled it up to save for posterity. The toad went over fairly well, and I even got a couple of laughs out of it, which is about all you can expect from a toad. Even so, Miss Deets chose not to compliment me on my performance. She just sat there slumped in her chair, fanning herself with a sheaf of arithmetic papers. I thought she looked a tad green, but that could have been my imagination.

Now only Margaret Fisher and Crazy Eddie were left to do their Show and Tells. I knew Eddie was planning to use several pig organs from a recent butchering, provided they hadn't spoiled too much by the time he got to use them. But Margaret changed his plans.

She brought in a cardboard box and proudly carried it to the front of the room. Miss Deets backed off to a far corner, her hands fluttering nervously about her mouth, as Margaret pried up the lid of the box. A mother cat and four cute baby kittens stuck out their heads. Everyone *ooh*ed and *aah*ed. Miss Deets went over and picked up one of the kittens and told Margaret what a wonderful idea she had had, to bring in the kittens, and would Margaret like to clean the blackboard erasers at recess?

At recess, Eddie was frantic. "I can't use the pig stuff now," he said. "I got to come up with something live that has cute babies."

"How about using Henry?" I suggested.

"Yeah, Henry's cute, all right, but he don't have no babies."

"Hey, I've got an idea!" I said. "I know some things we can use and just *say* they're his babies. But you'd better call Henry a girl's name. Heck, Miss Deets won't know the difference."

Eddie smiled. I knew he was thinking he would

soon have back his old job of cleaning the blackboard erasers for Miss Deets.

Everyone in third grade counted on Crazy Eddie Muldoon to come up with a spectacular grand finale for Show and Tell. An air of great expectation filled the room as Eddie, carrying a lard pail, marched up to make his presentation. Even Miss Deets seemed to be looking forward to the event, possibly because it was the last Show and Tell, but no doubt also because she expected one of her favorite pupils to come up with something memorable.

With the flair of the natural showman, Eddie deftly flipped off the lid of the lard pail, in which he had punched air holes. "And now, ladies and gentlemen," he announced, "here is Henrietta Muldoon . . . my pet garter snake." He held up the writhing Henry.

Miss Deets sucked in her breath with such force she stirred papers on desks clear across the room.

"And that's not all," Crazy Eddie continued, although it was plain from the look on Miss Deets's face that Henry all by himself was excessive. Beaming, Eddie thrust his other hand into the pail.

"Here, ladies and gentlemen, are her babies!"

He held up the squirming mass of nightcrawlers we had collected the evening before.

At first I thought the sound was a distant wail of a fire siren, a defective one, with a somewhat higher pitch than normal. It rose slowly and steadily in volume, quavering, piercing, until it vibrated the glass in the windows and set every hair of every third-grader straining at its follicle. We were stunned to learn that human vocal cords could produce such an unearthly sound, and those of a third-grade teacher at that.

Mr. Cobb, the principal, came and led Miss Deets away, and we never saw her again. We heard later that she had gone back to teach school in the city, where all the kids were rich and she could lead a peaceful and productive life.

As the door closed behind her, I turned to Eddie and said, "I think you've cleaned your last blackboard eraser for Miss Deets."

"Yeah, I suspect you're right," he said sadly. Then he brightened. "But you got to admit that was one whale of a Show and Tell!"

11

Not Long for This Whirl

AS AT THE BEGINNING of every spring in our part of the country, water invaded the world and ruled over it with a cold and merciless hand. It drizzled out of the murky sky, oozed up from the saturated ground, and roared in torrents from the melting snow in the mountains, filling the creek and river channels to overflowing, washing out bridges, pump houses, and any other structure within its grasp. Water that could find nothing more enterprising to do with itself turned the dirt roads of the country into sloughs of mud the color and consistency of butterscotch pudding.

It was not a fun time for a teenage outdoorsman. More or less trapped in the close confines of our farmhouse with my mother, grandmother, and sister (the Troll), I grew increasingly frustrated and irritable that my weekend had been washed out by the water. Seeing her chance, my grandmother rushed to aggravate my sorry state of mind.

"Your grandpap wouldn't let a little water keep him all wrapped up in the house like a festering sore, I can tell you that!" Gram said smugly, barely containing her glee. "He'd be out there right now, cutting down trees and skidding 'em to the mill. I can't even get you to go cut a pile of kindlin' wood. Nope, your grandpap shore wouldn't let a little water keep him in the house."

"Yeah, I can see why," I said meanly, trying to cut right to the quick. But Gram had tough quick and a stirring spoon with which she bonked me on top of the head.

"You're practically as worthless as that old reprobate Rancid Crabtree," she probed. "I ain't seen hide nor hair of him since the melt came, which is one good thing. You and him are both pantywaists, lettin' a little dampness make you hole up by the fire like a couple of sick pups."

"Arrrrh!" I yelled, bringing a burst of delight to Gram's face. "I am not a pantywaist, whatever that is. And besides, Rance is sick. He says he's dying."

Gram activated her scoff to full power. "You believe that? Well, let me tell you, Crabtree is too mean and ornery and dirty and smelly to die. And he's so lazy, nobody could tell if he did. What ails him is probably somebody offered him a job and scared the old windbag so bad he took to his bed."

I yawned to show her how bored I was with the debate, but I hoped Gram was right. My heart had welled with grief ever since the old woodsman told me, "Ah ain't long fer this whirl." I assumed he meant "world," but on the other hand he loved a good whirl as much as any man I've ever known, so I couldn't be sure. Rancid had taught me everything I knew about woodcraft, hunting and fishing and trapping and numerous other manly arts. Now my mentor in all things I valued most seemed to be dying. I had hesitated for several days even to visit him, for fear I might find him dead. Gram's subtle attempt to cheer me up had helped a little. I began to accumulate enough gumption—one of Gram's favorite words—to make a watery trek to the Crabtree shack, just to see if Rancid still lingered among the living.

"Why don't you heat up some of that chicken noodle soup we had for supper?" I said to Gram. "Maybe I'll take some over to Rancid. It can't make him any sicker than he already is."

"You think I'm going to waste good soup on old Crabtree, you must be tetched in the head!" Rancid was not one of Gram's favorite *Homo sapiens*, or even, for that matter, vertebrates. She stomped off to the kitchen, muttering to herself.

Turning back to the window, I practiced my melancholy stare, getting it perfected for the time I became a writer. All writers have melancholy stares, because they have seen so much misery. I couldn't wait to leave home so that I could start seeing misery.

Through the sheets of rain, I noticed a cloud of smoke moving down the mud road toward our house. It was accompanied by a series of explosions, like a tiny war advancing across the country in search of a truce. I recognized the phenomenon immediately—Mrs. Peabody. Mrs. Peabody was a mountain car that my friend Retch Sweeney and I had built ourselves and named after our favorite high school teacher.

Retch sloshed up the walk to our door. "You ain't gonna believe this," he said. "But I got Mrs. Peabody with me."

"I know that," I said. "I'm not blind and deaf, you know."

"I mean the first Mrs. Peabody, our teacher!"

I wouldn't have believed it, either, except for the beaming of Retch's big ugly face with the rain dribbling off the wispy chin-whiskers. As Retch hurriedly explained, Mrs. Peabody had telephoned the

Sweeney house and asked Retch if he could drive her out to a friend's house in the country, where she had been invited for the weekend. With the roads so bad, she said, she thought it would be safer if she had a man drive her. I guessed that she hadn't been able to find a man, so she called Retch. Although Retch probably could have borrowed the family sedan for such an important mission, he thought this would be a good opportunity to show off the mountain car to Mrs. Peabody.

"Want to go along?" Retch asked me. "Mrs. Peabody's friend lives up past the Market Road junction. Shouldn't take more than an hour both ways."

"Hey, Gram," I yelled. "I'm going out with Retch. I'll have him drop me off at Rancid's to see how he's doing. You don't mind, do you, Retch?"

"Naw. That road up to Crabtree's will really show Mrs. Peabody what the mountain car can do."

"Well, you just hold your horses," Gram yelled, "till I get this hot soup poured in a jug."

Gram poured the soup in a little crockery whiskey jug we kept in the kitchen for decoration. I thought Rancid would probably appreciate the appropriateness of the container, since he had several just like it that he didn't use for decoration.

Mrs. Peabody sat hunched over in her namesake,

a bit of wet hair plastered to her forehead. "How do you like our mountain car, Mrs. Peabody?" I asked, climbing in beside her.

"Oh, it's fine, fine," she said. "Quite lovely."

"I thought you'd like it," I said. "Retch and I built it ourselves."

"Really? I never would have guessed."

"Yep, what we did was, we left off everything that wasn't essential, like fenders and the exhaust pipe and muffler."

"And seats," she said, smiling tightly.

"Yeah, well, actually we couldn't find any seats. I hope that apple box isn't uncomfortable."

"Good heavens, no! Shall we go now, boys? The fumes in here are beginning to corrode my nasal passages."

"Wasn't me," Retch blurted.

"The exhaust fumes," I said. "That's one of the reasons we didn't put any windows on the car. The fumes dissipate to the outside. How'd you like the way I tossed in that vocabulary word, Mrs. Peabody—'dissipate'?"

"Very nice," she said, wiping a drop of water from the tip of her nose. "Very nice."

"Did you know we named the car after you?"

"Yes, I know," she said. "It's a rare honor."

I noticed a distinct lack of enthusiasm on the

part of Mrs. Peabody when I asked Retch to swing by Rancid's shack so I could drop off the jug of soup. Her lack of enthusiasm became even more pronounced as we started slipping and sliding down the mud road that led to the Sand Creek bridge.

"Stop! Stop!" she shrieked. "There's no bridge! No —— bridge!"

Later, Retch and I vaguely recalled that Mrs. Peabody had inserted into her shriek a bad word, but decided that couldn't possibly have been the case, she being a teacher.

Retch and I laughed. "Sure, there's a bridge," Retch said. "You just can't see it because it's about a foot underwater. Now I got to stop talking, so I can concentrate on exactly where the bridge is supposed to be, 'cause I sure wouldn't want to miss it. Har dee har!"

The mountain car crept slowly across the flooded bridge, the current trying to get a hold on the vehicle and hurl it and us into the maelstrom. Mrs. Peabody snatched a cigarette out of her purse and lit it with a trembling hand.

"I didn't know you smoked," I said, smoking not being common among the ladies I knew at that time.

"Only on occasion," she said. "This happens to be one of the occasions."

Having safely traversed the bridge, we ran out of luck on the steep slope of mud leading up the hill to Rancid's shack. Its tires spinning wildly, the mountain car suddenly lurched sideways into a ditch of rushing water, where it stuck fast.

Mrs. Peabody heaved a sigh that could have knocked a bird off a fence post, if the bird had been stupid enough to be out in the driving rain. "What'll we do now?" she asked, her voice quavering only slightly.

"No problem," I said. "I'll go get my friend Rancid Crabtree and have him tow us out with his truck. I just hope he's not dead yet, because then we'll be in a real fix."

"Dead?" Mrs. Peabody said, digging frantically in her purse for another cigarette. "What do you mean, dead?"

I didn't waste any time explaining, because the car seemed to be sinking deeper into the ditch by the second.

Splattered with mud halfway to my neck, I bounded through Rancid's door.

"Knock! Knock!" he croaked, his hand reaching for a shotgun beside the bed. "How many times Ah got to tell you?"

He didn't look well, wrapped up with a blanket all the way to his stubbly chin. His energy seemed drained out of him by the long winter, the watery spring, and, of course, his fatal illness.

"Good," I said. "You're not dead yet."

"Not yet," he growled feebly. "Ah'm gettin' thar, though."

I held up the whiskey jug of chicken noodle soup. "Look here! I brought you a little something."

Rancid's face broke into his big, snaggletoothed grin. "My, my! Ah knew thar was some reason Ah let you hang out with me all these y'ars. Mighty thoughtful of you. Now hand me thet jug. Iffen Ah got to die, Ah might jist as well die happy."

"Don't you want a bowl and spoon?" I asked. "It's chick—"

Rancid tilted the jug back and took a big swig. His eyes popped wide in horror. A huge shudder convulsed his body, and he spat the chicken noodle soup from one side of the shack to the other. "Goldang a-mighty!" he cried. "It's spiled! It's got dead worms in it!"

"No, it's not spoiled," I said. "It's not whiskey, for gosh sakes. It's chicken noodle soup. Gram sent it."

"Ah shoulda known!" he said. "Why, thet ornery old she-critter. I wasn't dyin' fast enough to suit her, so she put thet soup in a whiskey jug to disappoint me to death."

I quickly explained about the stuck mountain

car to Rancid and suggested that he tow us out with his truck. "I hate to bother you while you're dying, but we've got to get the car out."

"Cain't," Rancid said, taking a tentative sip of the soup. "Ah'm too sick. Jist leave her be till the ground dries out. Thet's what Ah'd do."

"I know. But we got our teacher, Mrs. Peabody, in the car," I pleaded. "She can't wade through mud all the way back to our house."

A thoughtful expression came over Rancid's face. "This Mrs. Peabody, what's she look like?" Even fatally ill, Rancid still had a strong interest in good-looking women, a promising sign.

"She's beautiful," I said, without lying much.

"Whar's Mr. Peabody?"

"I don't think there is one. I never ever heard him mentioned."

"Hmmmmmm," Rancid said. "Mebbe Ah could tow you out. This hyar soup seems to be bringin' some of maw strangth back."

He whipped off the blankets and climbed out of bed, fully clothed right down to his boots.

"You don't take your clothes off when you go to bed sick?" I asked.

"What fer?" he said. "If Ah got well, Ah'd jist have to put 'em back on again."

It made sense to me.

After much fussing around, finding chains and

ropes and Rancid's cranking his old truck to life, we arrived back at the scene of the accident. He parked the truck at the top of the hill, since he didn't want to get it stuck, too. If he didn't die right away, he said, he might need the truck again before the mud dried out. Rancid slogged down the hill and peered in at the huddled forms of Retch and Mrs. Peabody—particularly Mrs. Peabody, I was sure, because he had told me many times he had seen all he ever wanted to see of Retch.

"Howdy, ma'am," he said. "What seems to be the trouble here?"

It was a dumb thing to say, since any fool could see what the trouble was. I knew Rancid was just making conversation, even if Mrs. Peabody didn't. From the look on her face, I suspected she doubted the solution to the problem had just arrived.

"We're stuck," Mrs. Peabody said.

"Yep, and pretty good, Ah'd say. Ah'll tell you what we's got to do hyar. You and the animal has got to git out of the car, 'cause maw truck won't pull it out with you in it."

I poked Rancid in the back. "You don't expect Mrs. Peabody to wade in mud all the way up to her knees, do you?"

"Nope. Ah'll carry her up the hill and put her in maw truck."

"Uh, you think that's wise, you dying and all?"

"Sheddep and mind your own bidness."

At that moment, I realized that Rancid possessed the soul of a romantic, and that right here, on a mud-choked, rainsplattered mountain road in a remote corner of Idaho, chivalry was about to be resuscitated by a grizzled old woodsman. I was embarrassed.

As soon as the plan was explained to Mrs. Peabody, Rancid scooped her up in his arms and, ignoring her embarrassed protests, began tromping heavily up the slope to his truck. I soon ascertained that Mrs. Peabody was a bit plumper, the distance to the truck greater, and the mud deeper than the old woodsman and judged.

To conceal the strain on him, Rancid began to hum: "Hmmmm mmmmm mmmmm." Presently, however, the hum turned into more of a rhythmic and sustained grunt: "Mmmmm mm mmunh uuunh UNNNNNGH UNNGH UNGH!" And slowly his shoulders began to cave in and his back to bend, with Mrs. Peabody swaying precariously above and ever closer to the mud that sought to claim her.

"You're dropping meeee!" Mrs. Peabody wailed.

With a herculean effort and a hideous groan, Rancid wrenched the lady back up and plodded on, his boots making great long sucking sounds with every slow step he took in the mud. My teacher looked as if she was on the verge of hysteria, and I began to wonder how this might affect my grade in sophomore English. I also wondered if what I was witnessing might qualify as a misery, just in case I ever wanted to write about it.

At last Rancid reached the truck, and plopped Mrs. Peabody on the seat. He collapsed on the running board, alternating between wheezing and sucking in great gasps of air.

"Well, thank goodness," Mrs. Peabody said. "I certainly never thought we would make it. I did get some mud splattered on my coat, but it will probably brush right off when it dries. Now maybe you should hurry and get the car out of the ditch, Mr. Crabapple."

"Wheeeeze GASP Wheeeeze GASP," Rancid replied.

Presently, he pushed himself up and started dragging the heavy logging chain back down the hill to the mountain car. After a good deal of work, we finally got the chain hooked up and the car pulled out of the ditch, turned around, and headed back in the direction of the invisible bridge.

Rancid and I unhooked the tow chain and tossed it in back of the truck.

"Well, all that's left to do now is carry Mrs. Peabody back down to the car," I said. "Maybe you should just let her walk, you dying and all. I think my grade in English is already shot anyway, so it wouldn't hurt much."

"Nope," Rancid said. "Ah wouldn't feel right, let-tin' her walk through this slop. What a man's gotta do, a man's gotta do, even if he is dyin'."

"I'm ready for another ride," Mrs. Peabody called. "But please do try to be more careful this time."

"Yes, ma'am," Rancid said. Suddenly he turned and staggered backwards up to the door of the truck, where Mrs. Peabody stood on the running board. He bent over and put his hands on his knees. He seemed to be suffering some kind of attack. The exertions of carrying Mrs. Peabody and towing the car out of the ditch had taken their toll on him, and now seemed to be hastening his departure from this whirl even sooner than he'd expected. I was al-most paralyzed with shock and grief.

"Good heavens!" cried Mrs. Peabody. "Are you all right, Mr. Crabapple?"

"Ah ain't exactly feelin' chipper, if thet's what you mean," Rancid said. "So Ah'd 'preciate it if you'd climb aboard before Ah sink any deeper in the mud."

It was astonishing. In one afternoon I had seen chivalry suddenly reborn and just as suddenly snuffed out again. And chivalry was not the only thing snuffed out. Watching Rancid carry my English teacher piggyback down the hill to the mountain car, where the genetic accident known as Retch Sweeney howled in delight, I knew for certain that my slight hope of ever passing sophomore English had also just expired.

Tagging along behind Rancid and his human backpack, I could not help but feel sorry for Mrs. Peabody. All she had wanted was to be driven out to her friend's home in the country, where the two dignified ladies would spend the day sipping tea and discussing great literature. Now here she was, suffering the humiliation of being carried piggyback through the mud and rain by a smelly old mountain man. Rancid turned and backed up so that Mrs. Peabody could dismount into the open doorway of the car. I braced myself for the lash of sarcasm for which Mrs. Peabody was famous.

But to my astonishment, she was laughing. She held out her hand to the dumbfounded mountain man. "Rancid, you dear man," she said. "That was wonderful! I haven't ridden piggyback since I was a little girl! How can I thank you for all you've done?"

Rancid made some strange sound as he tried to untie his tongue.

"Oh, I'll tell you what," Mrs. Peabody went on. "I'll have you over to my house for tea. I'll bet you're a wonderful conversationalist."

"Yup," Rancid said.

Retch cranked up the mountain car's engine. Mrs. Peabody, coughing only slightly, stuck her head out of a cloud of exhaust smoke. "Remember the tea, Rancid. I'll give you a call."

The rain had stopped. Rancid and I waved at the departing mountain car, he thinking he was waving good-bye to a new lady friend and I knowing I was waving good-bye to a passing grade in sophomore English.

All at once, the sun broke through and set all the water and even the mud to gleaming as far as the eye could see. The new buds in the birch trees sparkled like emeralds, the mountains emerged from mists, and somewhere off in a meadow, a lark warbled.

"Shucks, Ah feels pretty good," Rancid said, grinning his snaggletoothed grin. "Ah reckon Ah won't die after all." His grin vanished. "Dang it! That Miz Peabody didn't ask for maw number!"

"Even if she had asked for your number, Rancid, it wouldn't do any good. You don't have a phone."

"Ah knows that, but she don't. Probably when she tries to call me and Ah don't answer, she'll write me a letter." His grin revived.

"Yeah," I said. "She'll probably write you a letter."

I chose not to remind Rancid that he didn't have an address, either.

12

The Night the Bear Ate Goombaw

THERE WAS SO MUCH CONFUSION over the incident anyway that I don't want to add to it by getting the sequences mixed up. First of all—and I remember this clearly—it was the summer after Crazy Eddie Muldoon and I had been sprung from third grade at Delmore Blight Grade School. The Muldoons' only good milk cow died that summer, shortly after the weasel got in their chicken house and killed most of the laying hens. This was just before the fertilizer company Mr. Muldoon worked for went bankrupt, and he lost his job. The engine on his tractor blew up a week later, so he couldn't harvest his crops, which were all pretty much dried up from the drought anyway.

Then Mr. Muldoon fell in the pit trap that Crazy Eddie and I had dug to capture wild animals. Our plan was to train the wild animals and then put on shows to earn a little extra money for the family. But Mr. Muldoon fell in the trap, and afterwards made us shovel all the dirt back into it. The only wild animal we had trapped was a skunk, and when Mr. Muldoon fell in on top of it, he terrified the poor creature practically to death. Neither Mr. Muldoon nor the skunk was hurt much, but the skunk managed to escape during all the excitement. So there went our wild-animal show. This occurred about midsummer, as I recall, about the time Mr. Muldoon's nerves got so bad that old Doc Hix told him to stop drinking coffee, which apparently was what had brought on his nervous condition.

For the rest of the summer, Mr. Muldoon gave off a faint, gradually fading odor of skunk. Unless he got wet. Then the odor reconstituted itself to approximately its original power, which placed a major restraint on the Muldoons' social life, meager as that was. Fortunately, Mr. Muldoon didn't get wet that often, mainly because of the drought that had killed off his crops. As Mrs. Muldoon was fond of saying, every cloud has a silver lining.

So far it had been a fairly typical summer for Mr. Muldoon, but he claimed to be worried about a premonition that his luck was about to turn bad. Then Eddie's grandmother, Mrs. Muldoon's mother, showed up for a visit.

"I knew it!" Mr. Muldoon told a neighbor. "I knew something like this was about to happen! I must be physic."

After I got to know Eddie's grandmother a little better, I could see why Mr. Muldoon regarded her visit as a stroke of bad luck. She immediately assumed command of the family and began to boss everyone around, including me. Nevertheless, I doubted that Mr. Muldoon was actually physic, because otherwise he would never have come up with the idea of the camping trip.

"I'm worried about Pa," Eddie said one morning as we sat on his back porch. "He's not been hisself lately."

"Who's he been?" I asked, somewhat startled, although I regarded Mr. Muldoon as one of the oddest persons I knew.

"Pa's just started acting weird, that's all. You know what crazy idea he came up with this morning? He says we all gotta go on a camping trip up in the mountains and pick huckleberries. He says we can sell any extra huckleberries we get for cash. But Pa don't know anything about camping. We don't even have any camping stuff. Ain't that strange?"

"Yeah," I said. "Say, Eddie, you don't suppose your pa . . . uh . . . your pa . . ." I tried to think of a delicate way to phrase it.

"What?" Eddie said.

"Uh, you don't suppose your pa, uh, would let me go on the camping trip too, do you?"

When Eddie put the question to his father, Mr. Muldoon tried to conceal his affection for me beneath a malevolent frown. "Oh, all right," he growled at me. "But no mischief. That means no knives, no hatchets, no matches, no slingshots, and *no shovels!* Understood?"

Eddie and I laughed. It was good to see his father in a humorous mood once again.

I rushed home and asked my mother if I could go camping with the Muldoons. "You'd be away from home a whole week?" she said. "I'll have to think about that. Okay, you can go."

I quickly packed my hatchet, knife, and slingshot, along with edibles Mom gave me to contribute to the Muldoon grub box. The one major item I lacked was a sleeping bag. "I'll just make a bedroll out of some blankets off my bed," I informed my mother.

"You most certainly won't," she informed me. "You'll use the coat."

"Ah, gee, Ma, the coat's so stupid. Mr. Muldoon will tease me all during the trip if I have to use that stupid coat for a sleeping bag."

The coat in question was a tattered, dog-chewed old fur of indeterminate species that my grandmother had acquired during a brief period of family wealth in the previous century. It had been given to me as a "sleeping bag" for my frequent but always aborted attempts at sleeping out alone in the yard. For all its hideous appearance, it was warm and cozy, and covered my nine-year-old body nicely from end to end. Still, I knew the Muldoons would laugh themselves silly when they saw me bed down in a woman's fur coat. My only hope of retaining a shred of dignity, not to mention my carefully nursed macho image, was to slip into it after they had all gone to sleep. I stuffed the coat into a gunnysack, concealing it under the one threadbare blanket my mother reluctantly issued me.

The day of the big camping trip dawned bright and clear, a common ruse of Mother Nature to lure unsuspecting souls out into the wilds. The five of us piled into the ancient Muldoon sedan and set off for the mountains. Most of our camping gear, such as it was, balanced precariously atop the car. It was wrapped in a huge hay tarp, which was to serve as our tent. "Ain't had a drop of rain in three months," Mr. Muldoon had said. "Probably won't need the tarp." This statement would later be recalled and admitted as evidence in the case against Mr. Muldoon's being physic.

"How you doin' back there, Goombaw?" Mr. Muldoon said to Eddie's grandmother. For some reason, everyone called her Goombaw.

"How you think I'm doin'?" Goombaw snapped back. "Wedged in between these two sweaty young-uns! I'm boilin' in my own juice! This camping trip is the stupidest dang fool idear you ever come up with, Herbert! We'll probably all get et by bears. Tell me, what about bears, Herbert?"

Yeah, I thought. What about bears?

"Ha ha ha ha," Mr. Muldoon laughed. "You don't have to worry about bears. They're more afraid of humans than we are of them."

Well, I thought, that's certainly not true of all humans, particularly one that I know personally. It's probably not true of all bears either. But I kept these thoughts to myself, since Goombaw was doing a thorough job of grilling Mr. Muldoon on the subject. I could tell that the talk of bears was making Mrs. Muldoon nervous, not that she was the only one.

"Let's change the subject, Goombaw," she said.

"Oh, all right. How about mountain lions, Herbert?"

For the rest of the long, hot, dusty ride up to the huckleberry patches, Goombaw harangued Mr. Muldoon about every possible threat to our well-being, from bears to crazed woodcutters. By the time we reached our campsite, she had everyone in such a nervous state that we were almost afraid to get out of the car. Mr. Muldoon stepped out, swiveled his head about as though expecting an attack from any quarter, and then ordered us to help set up camp.

No level area for our tent was immediately apparent, but Crazy Eddie and I finally located one. It was down a steep bank and on the far side of a little creek. Mr. Muldoon, Eddie, and I dragged the bundle of camp gear down the bank and across a log to the little clearing in the brush and trees. In no time at all Mr. Muldoon had constructed a fine shelter out of the tarp. Eddie and I built a fire ring of rocks, and Mrs. Muldoon and Goombaw got a fire going and put coffee on to boil, apparently forgetting that the doctor had told Mr. Muldoon to cut down on his coffee drinking because of his nerves. Eddie and I sampled the fishing in the creek. All in all, the camping trip showed signs of becoming a pleasant experience. Then it got dark.

"I say keep a fire goin' all night," Goombaw advised. "It might help keep the bears off of us."

"There ain't no bears," Mr. Muldoon said. "Now stop worrying about bears. Ha! Bears are more afraid of us than we are of them. Now, everybody get a good night's sleep. We got a lot of huckleberries to pick tomorrow." He stripped down to his long underwear and burrowed into the pile of quilts and blankets Mrs. Muldoon had arranged on the ground.

I pulled my threadbare blanket out of the gunny-sack and spread it out in the dirt next to Goombaw.

"Good heavens, Patrick!" Mrs. Muldoon said. "Is that all you have to sleep in, that one little blanket? The nights can get pretty chilly up here in the mountains."

"Oh, I've got more blankets in my sack," I lied. "If it turns cold, I'll just put some more on. But I sleep warm."

As the night dragged on into its full depth, I lay there shivering in my blanket, studying with considerable interest the looming dark shapes the full moon revealed around our camp. Finally, Goombaw and the Muldoons ceased their thrashing about on the hard ground and began to emit the sounds of sleep. I jerked the fur coat out of the gunnysack and buttoned myself into its comforting warmth. I set a mental alarm to awaken me before the Muldoons, so I could conceal the coat before they caught sight of the hideous thing. Then I drifted off into fitful sleep.

"Wazzat?" Goombaw shouted in my ear.

Later, she claimed only to be having a nightmare, but, fortunately for us, she sounded the alarm just in time. In the silence that followed Goombaw's shout, you could almost hear four pairs of eyelids popping open in the dark.

"A bear!" Goombaw shouted. "A bear's got me!"

Since I was lying right next to Goombaw, this announcement aroused my curiosity no end. I tried to leap to my feet but, wrapped in the fur coat, could only manage to make it to all fours.

"Bear!" screamed Crazy Eddie. "Bear's got Gooooo—!"

"Bear!" shrieked Mrs. Muldoon. "There it is!"

Goombaw made a horrible sound. I could make out the big round whites of her eyes fixed on me in the darkness, no doubt pleading wordlessly with me for help, but what could a small boy do against a bear?

"Holy bleep!" roared Mr. Muldoon. He lunged to his feet, knocking over the ridgepole and dropping the tarp on us and the bear. Figuring Goombaw already for a goner and myself next on the bear's menu, I tore out from under the tarp just in time to see Mr. Muldoon trying to unstick an ax from the stump in which he had embedded it the night before. Even in the shadowy dimness of moonlight, I could see the look of surprise and horror wash over Mr. Muldoon's face as I rushed toward him for protection. He emitted a strangled cry and rushed off through the woods on legs so wobbly it looked as if his knees had come unhinged. Under the circumstances, I could only surmise that the bear was close on my heels, and I raced off after Mr. Muldoon, unable to think of anything better to do. With his abrupt departure, Mr. Muldoon had clearly let it be known that now it was every man for himself.

Bounding over a log with the effortless ease that accompanies total panic, I came upon Mr. Muldoon peeling bark and limbs off a small tree. Since he was only four feet up the tree, I debated briefly whether to wait for him to gain altitude or to find my own tree. Then Mr. Muldoon caught sight of the bear closing fast on us. He sprang out of the tree and took off again, with me so close behind that I could have reached out and grabbed the snapping flap of his long underwear. The thought did occur to me to do so, because I was nearing exhaustion, and Mr. Muldoon could have towed me along with his underwear flap. Upon later reflection, however, I think it is well that I didn't grab the flap, for it probably would have been a source of considerable embarrassment to both of us.

When I could run no more, I dropped to the ground, deciding I might as well let the bear eat me as run me to death. But the bear was gone. Perhaps he had taken a shortcut through the woods, hoping to cut me and Mr. Muldoon off at a pass. In any case, I never did get to see the bear, narrow as my escape had been. Sweltering in the fur coat, I took the thing off and stuffed it down a hollow stump, glad to be rid of the thing.

When I got back to camp, everyone was gone. I climbed up to the car, inside of which I found Eddie, his mother, and Goombaw, each more or less in one piece.

"Thank heavens," cried Mrs. Muldoon. "We thought the bear had got you! Have you seen Mr. Muldoon?"

I said yes I had, not mentioning that I had seen even more of him than I cared to. Half an hour later, Mr. Muldoon scrambled up the bank to the car. Upon learning that everyone was intact, he explained how he had led the bear away from camp, at considerable risk to himself. I was surprised that he neglected to mention my role in leading the bear off, but didn't think it my place to mention it.

"You got to keep a cool head during a bear attack," Mr. Muldoon explained. "Panic and you're done for."

"Wheweee!" Goombaw said. "I smell skunk! Somebody step on a skunk in the dark?"

Then it started to rain. Hard.